ARE THEY WOMEN?

broadview editions
series editor: Martin R. Boyne

ARE THEY WOMEN?
A NOVEL CONCERNING
THE THIRD SEX

Aimée Duc

[Mina Adelt-Duc]

edited and translated by Margaret Sönser Breen
and Nisha Kommattam

broadview editions

BROADVIEW PRESS – www.broadviewpress.com
Peterborough, Ontario, Canada

Founded in 1985, Broadview Press remains a wholly independent publishing house. Broadview's focus is on academic publishing; our titles are accessible to university and college students as well as scholars and general readers. With 800 titles in print, Broadview has become a leading international publisher in the humanities, with world-wide distribution. Broadview is committed to environmentally responsible publishing and fair business practices.

© 2020 Margaret Sönser Breen and Nisha Kommattam

Library and Archives Canada Cataloguing in Publication

Title: Are they women? : a novel concerning the third sex / Aimée Duc (Mina Adelt-Duc) ; edited and translated by Margaret Sönser Breen and Nisha Kommattam.
Other titles: Sind es Frauen?. English
Names: Duc, Aimée, 1869-approximately 1908, author. | Breen, Margaret Sönser, editor, translator. | Kommattam, Nisha, editor, translator.
Series: Broadview editions.
Description: Series statement: Broadview editions | Translation of: Sind es Frauen?. | Includes bibliographical references.
Identifiers: Canadiana (print) 20200295608 | Canadiana (ebook) 20200295616 | ISBN 9781554814800 (softcover) | ISBN 9781770487901 (PDF) | ISBN 9781460407417 (EPUB)
Classification: LCC PT2607.U26 S5613 2020 | DDC 833/.91—dc23

Broadview Editions
The Broadview Editions series is an effort to represent the ever-evolving canon of texts in the disciplines of literary studies, history, philosophy, and political theory. A distinguishing feature of the series is the inclusion of primary source documents contemporaneous with the work.

Advisory editor for this volume: Colleen Humbert

Broadview Press handles its own distribution in North America:
PO Box 1243, Peterborough, Ontario K9J 7H5, Canada
555 Riverwalk Parkway, Tonawanda, NY 14150, USA
Tel: (705) 743-8990; Fax: (705) 743-8353
email: customerservice@broadviewpress.com

For all territories outside of North America, distribution is handled by Eurospan Group.

Broadview Press acknowledges the financial support of the Government of Canada for our publishing activities.

Typesetting and assembly: True to Type Inc., Claremont, Canada
Cover Design: Lisa Brawn

PRINTED IN CANADA

To Anni

Contents

Acknowledgements

We are indebted to so many people and organizations. They have not only provided us with documents and advice but also shown us enthusiasm, generosity, and kindness.

We would like to thank the numerous feminist, lesbian, and other institutions in Germany and France that have aided us in our research, particularly with regard to Adelt-Duc's biography. They are as follows: the Stiftung des Archivs zur deutschen Frauenforschung in Kassel (ADDF), in particular Dr. Mirjam Sachse, and their tremendously helpful online databank; the Bildungszentrum und Archiv zur Frauengeschichte Baden-Württembergs in Tübingen (baf e.V.); the Feministische Bibliothek Monaliesa Leipzig; the Frauenforschungs, -bildungs und -informationszentrum Berlin (FFBIZ e.V.); the Institut für Deutsche Presseforschung, Universität Bremen and Dr. Stephanie Seul; the Frauen Media Turm in Cologne and Ellen Hanisch; Auszeiten e.V. in Bochum and Rita Kronauer; the Institut für Zeitungsforschung in Dortmund and Gudrun Paladini; Spinnboden Lesbenarchiv e.V. and Katja Koblitz; the Zentrum für transdisziplinäre Geschlechterstudien (ZtG) at Humboldt Universität zu Berlin and Dr. Karin Aleksander; the university archive at TU Dortmund and Stephanie Marra; Belladonna e.V. in Bremen and Julia Chaker; the Zentralarchiv Evangelische Kirche in Hessen und Nassau, and Sabine Hübner; Stadtarchiv Jena, in particular Constanze Mann; Stadtarchiv Zürich, especially Patrick Kägi and Caroline Senn; and the Archives de la ville et de l'Eurométropole de Strasbourg, France, particularly Jérôme Ruch and Laurence Perry.

We are grateful to several libraries for the research support that they have provided: in Austria, the Österreichische Nationalbibliothek, especially Christa Bader-Reim, Romana Holtemayer, Ulrike Polnitzky, Veronika Wöber, and Eike Zimmer; in Germany, the Martin-Opitz-Bibliothek, Herne and the Staatsbibliothek Bamberg, in particular Otmar Singer and Fabian Bayer; in Switzerland, the Schweizerische Nationalbibliothek and the Zentralbibliothek Zürich; in the United States, the University of Chicago Library and especially the Homer D. Babbidge Library of the University of Connecticut, in particular Joe Natale and the Interlibrary Loan team, whose efforts on behalf of this project have been essential.

Many people have also aided us. We acknowledge the helpful conversations and work of the following individuals: Ulrich Adelt, Anke Finger, Alex Gatten, Katharina von Hammerstein, Martin Kimpel, Clare King'oo, Gregory Kneidel, Ludmilla Rieberer, Janice Robes, Robert D. Tobin, and Sarah Winter. Particular thanks go to Klaus Kaindl of the Universität Wien and Beatrice Fischer, whose March 2015 conference "Queering Translation, Translating the Queer," proved a catalyst for this project; Marina Bleiler, who translated and explained a key Russian phrase in *Are They Women?*; Dr. Ulrich Ecker, who provided us with substantial help by interpreting the Strasbourg archival documents regarding Adelt-Duc's family; the anonymous book vendor who kindly provided us with a digital image of the book cover to *Indische Novellen*; and Broadview's anonymous reviewers who endorsed our project.

In addition to Mara Taylor's 2010 dissertation, we also wish to acknowledge the pioneering intellectual contributions of Lillian Faderman, Claudia Schoppmann, Hanna Hacker, and Christiane Leidinger.

We are especially indebted to two individuals for the substantial support that they have provided us in our research. Richard Bleiler, Collections and Humanities Librarian of the University of Connecticut, contacted, on our behalf, any number of institutions in Austria, Germany, and the United States. Early on, he found a document that proved crucial to our uncovering of new biographical information regarding Adelt-Duc. Finally, research assistant Vinzent Ahlbach of the Universität zu Köln gathered a wealth of secondary critical material. We heartily acknowledge his work, supported by the German Federal Ministry of Education and Research.

Introduction

Reclaiming *Are They Women?* A Novel Concerning the Third Sex for Lesbian Literary History

Sind es Frauen? Roman über das dritte Geschlecht (hereafter *Are They Women? A Novel Concerning the Third Sex*) is little known in Germany, let alone in other countries, today. Written by popular German author and women's rights advocate Mina (or Minna) Adelt-Duc under her pseudonym Aimée Duc, the novel was published in 1901 by Richard Eckstein Nachfolger as part of that press's modern library series, *Ecksteins Moderne Bibliothek*. Two years earlier, Eckstein had released *Das dritte Geschlecht* (*The Third Sex*) by well-known writer Ernst von Wolzogen (1855–1934). That novel presented a satirical and contemptuous description of strong, independent women, whose emancipation was, by the end of the century, increasingly coded as lesbian. *Are They Women?* is Adelt-Duc's response. The text offers a lively portrait of lesbian university students and friends who trouble the gender norms of turn-of-the-nineteenth-century Central Europe because they claim the right both to higher education and to love other women. Lillian Faderman and Brigitte Eriksson have called *Are They Women?* "the most articulate German literary statement about lesbian life and feminist theory [of its] time" (vi). Why, then, did this novel initially meet with tepid reviews, and why has it since then continued to be critically overlooked?

In its ability to speak to key gender issues, *Are They Women?* was ahead of its time. In 1901, very few texts, literary or otherwise, provided a serious and positive consideration of lesbianism. With regard to same-sex desire, sexologists such as Richard von Krafft-Ebing (1840–1902) focused primarily on men. His groundbreaking *Psychopathia Sexualis* includes only a few case studies of lesbians, one of which, the case of Count Sandor or Countess V, inspired British novelist Radclyffe Hall (1880–1943) to write her landmark *The Well of Loneliness* (1928), whose tragic plot influenced generations of writers and readers of lesbian literature in English. *Are They Women?* had no such wide-ranging impact, in part because Adelt-Duc was not an established literary figure. Yet perhaps its dismissal was also the result of the novel's very strengths.

While *Are They Women?* is informed by contemporary sexological discussions, it offers readers a feminist and lesbian love story with a happy ending. The novel is short, and its writing style is readily accessible, as is its language, which avoids pathologizing medical terms. Anxiety and self-doubt do not overwhelm the characters. Instead, they rather easily celebrate the existence and viability of lesbian love, albeit a love that still remains discreet and fairly hidden. The protagonist may recognize that she and her friends belong to those "'Krafft-Ebing types'" (p. 78), but she is quick to explain the larger social significance of that identification: "we are the representatives of a mixture, a human species that, without exception manifesting itself as an intellectual elite, is entitled to consideration" (p. 58).

The novel's characters also assume the importance of affording women the opportunity to study; this position was a topical one. While the University of Zurich, Switzerland, had formerly begun admitting women as students in 1867, it was just in 1900, a year before the publication of the novel, that Baden became the first German state to allow women to enroll in university. Bavaria was next in 1903, and interestingly some of the novel's story takes place in Munich, where protagonist Minotschka attends university classes. In this instance it is unclear whether Adelt-Duc was anticipating the soon-to-be realized opening of Bavarian universities to women or whether she was simply minimizing the distinction between the admission of women and the permission that they had already obtained to audit courses. Her decision to set most of the novel outside of Germany—in the cities of Geneva and Paris—shields this question from direct national critique and in effect insulates her advocacy for women's access to higher education. So, a group of German men tell Minotschka and her friends in a chance encounter, "in our country, university-educated women are still a rarity" (p. 75).

Perhaps Adelt-Duc's success in transmitting hotly contested issues regarding women's rights and lesbianism so readily and in everyday, understandable language explains why early critics dismissed the novel. *Are They Women?* does not so much invite debate as foreclose it. Adelt-Duc's narrative strategy may well have proven unsettling.

Certainly, the novel is not aesthetically beautiful or well crafted. Nor is it subtle. While her main characters are vividly drawn and suggest her intimate knowledge of lesbian and feminist gatherings, Adelt-Duc offers characters who are more declarative than developed. She signals emotion and excitement—and in the novel there is a lot of both—through her free and ready use of exclamation marks. Her transitions are often abrupt. Even so, it would be a mistake to overlook the appeal of the novel, which lies in its accessibility for a general readership and its animated embrace of its subject matter. *Are They Women?* holds cultural, historical, and literary significance. Conversant in women's rights debates and discussions of the third sex, the novel speaks to the lively communities of lesbians in existence across turn-of-the-century Central Europe. It is one of the first lesbian novels written in German—and, for that matter, in any language. It is also one of the very few pre–Second Wave feminist texts, whether German or otherwise, to provide a positive, non-pathologizing, and romantic portrait of lesbians. As such, it complicates the dominant critical narrative of pre-liberation lesbian literature, whereby heroines conventionally face loneliness, imprisonment, madness, death, and heterosexual conversion. The novel may not be a work of high literature, but its popular appeal is undeniable. It is highly readable and remarkably progressive for its time.

Publication History

Are They Women? enjoyed a robust first-edition print run of 10,000 copies. It seems, however, to have garnered only modest critical attention (see Appendix A). *Westermanns Illustrierte Deutsche Monatshefte* (*Westermann's Illustrated German Monthly Magazine*) made brief mention of the novel, and that only in order to cast it as derivative, capitalizing on the success of Wolzogen's *Das dritte Geschlecht* (see Appendix A1). A more substantial review appeared in the *Jahrbuch für sexuelle Zwischenstufen* (hereafter *Yearbook for Intermediate Sexual Types*), published by sexologist and sexual rights advocate Magnus Hirschfeld (1868–1935) (see Appendix A2). There, the judgement was mixed. As a work of literature, the novel proved disappointing: "There is little substance to the narrative; nowhere are the themes and actions realised; the whole functions more as a sketch" (p. 101). It was, however, "comprised of interesting philosophical and socio-ethical discussions," whose concerns with women's rights Adelt-Duc's lesbian characters fittingly articulate: "The author strategically puts her reflections on women's emancipation into the mouths of homosexual women ... given that their nature and their more masculine character, will undoubtedly be the most prototypical representatives of women's rights" (p. 101). The novel, together with the next one, *Ich will!* (*I Do!*), later appeared in a three-author fiction anthology, *Erzählungen berühmter Autoren: Fritz Skowronnek, Otto Behrend,*

Aimée Duc (*Stories by Famous Authors: Fritz Skowronnek, Otto Behrend, Aimée Duc*).

Are They Women? was reintroduced to readers in the 1970s and 1980s. The German feminist press *Amazonen Frauen Verlag* (Verlag Gabriele Meixner) reissued the novel in 1976 and then, in 1980, Lillian Faderman and Brigitte Eriksson included a partial translation of the novel in their important collection, *Lesbian-Feminism in Turn-of-the-Century Germany*, published by Naiad Press. A Dutch translation of the novel, with which Faderman was also involved, appeared in 1984. Until now, no full English translation has been available. For more than thirty years, the novel has been out of print.

Mina Adelt-Duc (Aimée Duc): A Brief Biography

Who was the author of this pioneering, if overlooked, lesbian novel? For all her publications, relatively little is known for certain about businesswoman, journalist, editor, and novelist Mina Adelt-Duc.[1] An intriguing ambiguity, beginning with her name and cultural identification, surrounds her. In some sense, this ambiguity characterizes the New Woman, who questioned, negotiated, and transgressed traditional gender and sexual prescriptions within largely patriarchal contexts. Her various professional names bespeak a woman who resisted presenting a fixed public persona. Her commitment to personal as well as professional independence heightens the challenge of tracing out details of her life. Tantalizingly little is known about her, in part because of her successful negotiation of cultural and social barriers and because of her frequent crossings of geographical and political borders. As an adult she traveled widely in Europe, Western Asia, North Africa, the Indian subcontinent, and mainland Southeast Asia. She lived for more than twenty years in British-controlled India, including for the duration of World War I. After her return to Germany in 1926, little more is known of her. Adelt-Duc was a woman who, even as she enjoyed a successful professional life, continually broke with social conventions and narratives that might otherwise have kept track of her.

Cultural, political, and linguistic crossings are part of Adelt-Duc's family history. Born Hedwig Maria Mina Adelt in Breslau, Prussia, on 1 May 1867, she was raised and educated in the

---

1 Based on our original archival research, we offer the first extended discussion of Adelt-Duc's life and work.

border city of Strasbourg, where her family moved in 1873. Strasbourg, at the end of the Franco-Prussian War, had become part of Germany (only to become French again at the end of World War I). Her mother was Elise Duc (1832–1902). Her father, Ferdinand Adelt (1828–91), was a postal official born in Tilsit, East Prussia, another city characterized by multiple ethnicities and languages, including German, Lithuanian, Polish, and Russian. Adelt-Duc was the second of three children: a sister, Adeline, was born in 1862; a brother, Eduard Ferdinand, in 1876. The family seems to have been financially comfortable. Adelt-Duc was also evidently related to another German writer, Leonhard Adelt (1881–1945), to whom she dedicated her 1904 novel *Des Pastors Liebe. Ein modernes Sittenbild (The Pastor's Love. A Portrait of Modern Manners)*.

Adelt-Duc wrote in German, her prose sprinkled often with French as well as, occasionally, Russian expressions. In 1890, she moved to Berlin. While in the mid-1890s she also spent time in Munich and in Dresden, she lived primarily in Berlin through the turn of the century and there became active in the German women's movement. By the time she was in her thirties, she had added her mother's maiden name "Duc" to her surname. Over the course of her career, she published her work under various names: apart from the pseudonym Helvetia, which she apparently used early on, she also, during her marriage to Swiss journalist Oskar Wettstein (1866–1952) from 1889 until 1896, wrote under the name Wettstein-Adelt. While some of her articles continued to appear under that name a few years after the couple's divorce, the end of the marriage and consequent separation from her child, Maria Marta Aimée (1889–1918), mark the start of a new phase of self-definition. She began signing herself Mina—or M.A.—Adelt-Duc for public records, journalistic pieces, and selected works of non-fiction. For other non-fiction publications, and for her fiction and one theological pamphlet, she wrote as Aimée Duc, a name that foregrounds her maternal bond. It is not known whether Adelt-Duc had any further contact with her daughter, subsequently raised by Wettstein and his second wife; given the separation, if not estrangement and loss, the pen name seems especially poignant. Her many names and pseudonyms attest to how she sought to direct her own life as much as possible, despite the gender limitations imposed on women in the societies through which she moved. While she penned herself Wettstein-Adelt during her first marriage, it is significant that her publications after 1901 bear no sign of her second marriage and that, until now, no literary biographer or critic has made mention of it. She insisted on her personal and professional autonomy.

While Adelt-Duc's writings address a range of topical issues, many, if not most, of her publications engage questions central to and intersecting with the women's movement of late-nineteenth- and early-twentieth-century Germany: for example, working-class women's rights and living conditions, dress reform, the importance of physical culture, prostitution, children's welfare, women's access to both higher education and middle-class professions, women's equality, and questions regarding marriage and the third sex. She contributed to the movement through her roles as journalist, editor, and fiction writer: while her articles reported on these issues and her editorial work continually kept them before her readership, her longer work, both fiction and non-fiction, animated them.

By 1891, Adelt-Duc's writing career was underway. In that year she published the booklet *Des Hauses Tausendkünstler. Ein treuer Rathgeber für den Haushalt* (*The Household Wizard. A Faithful Guide for the Household*). The articles that followed over the next few years appeared in venues dedicated to women's issues or sociological interests, such as *Blatt der Hausfrau* (*The Homemaker's Newspaper*); *Blätter für soziale Praxis* (*Papers on Social Praxis*); and *Ethische Kultur* (*Ethical Culture*). These pieces reveal a consistent focus on the everyday concerns of working- and middle-class women and, increasingly, on women's rights. Her pamphlet *Macht euch frei! Ein Wort an die deutschen Frauen* (*Free Yourselves! A Word to German Women*), a convincing, if clumsily executed, argument against the evils of corsets, and her undercover account and practical study *3½ Monate Fabrik-Arbeiterin* (*Female Factory Worker for 3½ Months*) both appeared in 1893 and were published under the name Wettstein-Adelt.

The latter text cemented Adelt-Duc's reputation as a writer who was committed to the women's movement. Closely modeled on Paul Göhre's 1891 study of male factory workers, *3½ Monate* intimately describes the living and working conditions of female factory workers in turn-of-the-century Saxony. Her explicit motivation for this project was the advancement of the German women's movement among the working classes. By posing as a factory worker and concealing her own privileged background, she gained access to a stocking factory, a weaving mill, and a spinning mill over a period of several months and in some cases formed close bonds with workers. The study draws rather essentialist, biased stereotypes of the women whom she encountered, creating a problematic, hierarchized typology of the characteristics of various types of workers. For example, she argues that the more strenuous and unrefined the type of labor in question is, the more unrefined and vulgar the women performing such labor are. She also had much to say about the unhygienic living conditions afforded the women, and the consequent need not only for more public baths and basic cooking instruction but also for women doctors. Three narrative motifs permeate the text. The first is Adelt-Duc's agenda for the advancement and liberation of working-class women, and the second, her Marxist ideologies (both of these inform her political motivation); the third is her privileged class bias, which is strongly reflected in alternatingly patronizing and romanticizing analyses. Already cited in the 1890s by physician and social critic Max Nordau (1849–1923) in his second edition of *Entartung (Degeneration)*, *3½ Monate* has since then often been referenced, excerpted, and republished.

The year 1893 also marked the beginning of Adelt-Duc's role as editor of multiple publications. For example, from that year until 1900 she oversaw the magazine *Berliner Modenkorrespondenz (Berlin Fashion Correspondence)*; in her new capacity, she traveled across Germany and to Italy and France. In the following year, she edited *Für die Frau. Organ für die Interessen der Frauenwelt in Stadt und Land (For Women. A Voice for Women's Interests in Town and Country)* and appears to have directed its focus toward the role of women in a social democracy. Then, at the end of 1894, Adelt-Duc took on her most substantial journalistic project. After being named chair of Berlin's newly created *Damen-Radfahr-Verein* (Women's Cycling Association), she founded *Draisena. Blätter für Damenradfahren. Organ zur Pflege und Förderung des Radfahrens der Damen (Draisena. Newspaper for Women's Cycling. Voice for the Support and Promotion of Women's Cycling)* (see Appendix E). Issued biweekly, the magazine ran until January 1900 and was published in Dresden and eventually in Vienna as well; Adelt-Duc served as editor-in-chief through December 1899. *Draisena* became a venue for exploring many of the subjects coalescing around the metaphor of female mobility, subjects in which she in particular and New Women more generally were interested: sport, travel, photography, fashion, and women's rights. She included articles that, taking up the polemical topic of bloomers, praised women cyclists who donned pants for comfort, safety, style, and pleasure. There were also illustrations and descriptions of what might be termed early versions of the sports bra. In addition to offering advertisements for and descriptions of various kinds of bicycles, *Draisena* listed excursions and included short vignettes regarding cycling vacations throughout Europe and even Morocco and South Africa. Later issues also had advertisements for motor cars and for motoring associations, along with photographs of various cycling and motor organizations and of single women riders on touring and racing bikes. The latter photographs in particular feature some beautifully composed images of women.

With the turn of the century, Adelt-Duc began a new phase in her explorations of gender autonomy on professional, personal, and political levels. In 1900, she attended, as part of the Russian delegation, the Ninth Universal Peace Congress in Paris, held from 30 September to 5 October, and Paris is listed as her residence. While it is not clear why she was a member of this particular delegation, her positioning anticipates the bicultural ties of her fictional namesake Minotschka Fernandoff, the Franco-Russian heroine of *Are They Women?*, released some months afterwards. One of a number of late-nineteenth- and early-twentieth-century international meetings dedicated to pacifism, the Congress advocated for disarmament and international courts of justice. By the end of the nineteenth century, women's rights were a part of the Congress's platform. The Paris meeting witnessed a number of appeals on behalf of women—appeals that reflected a spirit of enlightened colonial Eurocentrism; various speakers called for the protection of European and indigenous women from violence and for the recognition of and the respect for the rights of colonized peoples, including support for women's education among Hindu and Muslim populations. It is not known in which discussions Adelt-Duc participated; even so, her writings after *Are They Women?* indicate an awareness of the lives of women from the Indian subcontinent.

For example, the characters in her 1902 novel *Ich will!* include an Indian-German woman who grew up in India and is a practicing Buddhist; an unmarried, well-to-do, gifted painter from a middle-class family in Heidelberg; and a free-spirited and jolly writer called Minna, who, playfully linked in both name and attitude to Adelt-Duc as well as to her earlier protagonist Minotschka, exhibits the cosmopolitan and carefree lifestyle of an unmarried world traveler. Whereas the Indian-German woman is an other-worldly and deeply melancholic character whose longing for death gestures toward the lack of social and narrative space afforded racially mixed women, Minna represents a wholly different type of unmarried, unattached woman: practical, high-spirited, talkative, creative, and adventurous, she travels around the world following journalistic assignments or literary projects. Her financial success as an author permits her to remain unmarried; her childfree status allows her to travel and enjoy life as she pleases. The painter, too, is an autonomous artist, and at first her life choices render her successful as well. But the strong-willed and unconventional opinions she holds about paternity and romantic love (she views both as entirely unnecessary) are not mirrored or respected by society, and thus they result in the tragic suicide of her only child, conceived out of wedlock. Focusing on women's lives outside the familiar frame of marriage, *Ich will!* offers another example of Adelt-Duc's exploration of New Woman concerns. Her depiction of passionate friendship, drawing together these three unique and unconventional characters in turn-of-the-century Germany, combines with a call for women's legitimacy apart from marriage, the latter demand encoded in the title itself.

By the summer of 1901, Adelt-Duc was in England, where she gathered materials for articles on English theater and the temperance question. There, she met Theodor Riebeling (1870–1959), a German Lutheran pastor. The two evidently lived together and then, on 14 September, married in a registry office in Birmingham. Significantly, she continued to sign her works as either Adelt-Duc or Aimée Duc. For his part, Riebeling, having been a pastor for two years at a German seamen's mission in London, gave up his position upon marrying her. He returned to it only in 1932, when he took over the duties of a parish that his father had served decades before. By 1903, Adelt-Duc, along with Riebeling, had left Europe and moved to Cairo. In 1904 she established a business, Asiatisch-Orientalische Industriekorrespondenz (Asiatic-Oriental Industry Correspondence), with offices in Damascus, Smyrna, Alexandria, Cairo, Bombay, Calcutta, Birmingham, and London. Around that time, she and Riebeling traveled to India and eventually settled in Calcutta, where they lived until 1926. Until the start of World War I, Adelt-Duc traveled widely throughout Western Asia, North Africa, the Indian subcontinent, and mainland Southeast Asia.

We know little about the circumstances of Adelt-Duc's second marriage, but the fact that she married again raises many questions. After all, her works consistently critique marriage and consider the ways in which women could define themselves apart from it. One might understandably think that, as a writer concerned with women's rights and with the recognition of the third sex, Adelt-Duc would have considered marriage anathema or, again, in the words of Countess Kinzey of *Are They Women?*, a "comedy of errors" (p. 58). Yet her biography, incomplete as it is, eludes easy narrativization. While there is no clear-cut explanation, given the autobiographical strands at work in her various publications it is possible that her 1904 novel *Des Pastors Liebe* provides some sense of the motivations behind her second marriage.

Most obviously, *Des Pastors Liebe*, a *Bildungsroman* that focusses on the intellectual, emotional, and social awakening of the title character, suggests that Adelt-Duc married for love. Moreover, with characters' names, professions, locations, and relationships all recalling her own personal life, she invites readers to understand that love as fundamentally feminist in its expression. The novel describes the complicated and turbulent romance between a German Lutheran pastor who struggles with his vocation and a well-traveled journalist and fiction writer. While they eventually marry in a civil ceremony, the writer's opposition to the institution initially leads to their living together in a free union without any religious or legal sanctioning of their bond. Grounded in friendship, theirs is a relationship between comrades, a form of intimate partnership promoted by the women's rights movement.

Des Pastors Liebe reflects Adelt-Duc's recurring concern for the ways in which women could enter into marriage and still maintain their personal and professional autonomy. Like her other works of fiction, the novel is artistically lacking. Yet even as its detailed dialogues on religious and societal hypocrisy, middle-class morality, and women's rights, including reproductive rights, are tedious, they allow her to emphasize the early-twentieth-century conflict between emerging feminist values and fading religious discourses. Moreover, she fashions the female protagonist as a brave, heroic, and morally superior character who educates and inspires the tender-hearted and somewhat naïve male protagonist. This reversal of conventional gender roles and consequent allocation of power, knowledge, and authority to a woman may suggest something of the terms of Adelt-Duc's own marriage. Perhaps her relationship with Riebeling can be understood as a strategic negotiation: at once an expression of free love rooted in comradeship and a marriage of convenience, designed to safeguard her desire to travel across colonial and non-European cultural and geographical spaces, where her status as a married woman might have offered her some degree of social mobility and protection.

The respective *oeuvres* of Adelt-Duc and Riebeling also suggest that the marriage, at least in its initial years, was shaped by personal pragmatism as well as feminist principles, whereby intellectual mutuality informed the writings of both. For example, the 1903 *Elternpflicht und Kindesrecht. Ein Beitrag zur freien Heiratswahl (Parental Duty and Children's Rights. A Contribution to the Issue of Autonomous Marital Choice)*, ostensibly authored by Riebeling, draws on the terminology and arguments of turn-of-the-century German feminism, which Adelt-Duc engages in her work. The favorably reviewed book identifies not only individual freedom and respect for individual personality but also sexual candor and love as foundational for successful marriages. In so doing, it rejects a blind adherence to social and religious practices and calls instead for a "radical moral renewal of the state of pastoral care."[1] Not parents but rather children themselves needed to choose their own partners. Part verbal nose-thumbing at parental and religious authority and part defense of marriage for love's sake, the text reads like the non-fiction companion piece to Adelt-Duc's novel *Des Pastors Liebe*, with its polemical treatment of the religious and social conventions regarding marriage and family. The two texts are also stylistically similar. By contrast, Adelt-Duc's next book, a pamphlet titled *Die Emmaus-Frage. Auch eine Kritik der reinen Vernunft (The Emmaus Question. Also a Critique of Pure Reason)*, which appeared in 1905, represents an intellectual, thematic, and stylistic departure from both Riebeling's text and Adelt-Duc's earlier publications. Called by one reviewer "curious" if nonetheless "instructive," it seems to have had members of the clergy and religious scholars as its intended readership. It is possible that Adelt-Duc actually wrote *Elternpflicht* and Riebeling *Die Emmaus-Frage*; at the very least a spirit of feminist collaboration and exchange characterizes the generation of these texts.

Once Adelt-Duc left Europe, her journalistic ventures had mixed success. Articles on crafts and trade in Cairo and Smyrna, which she wrote under the auspices of her business, Asiatisch-Orientalische Industriekorrespondenz, were criticized for their cursory discussion of issues. Her pieces on travel and photography fared better. The editorship of *Draisena*, which regularly fea-

---

1 Theodor Riebeling, *Elternpflicht und Kindesrecht. Ein Beitrag zur freien Heiratswahl* (Verlag der Frauen-Rundschau, 1903), 49.

tured photographs, had certainly prepared her for engaging this medium. Photography was also, by the end of the nineteenth century, a vehicle for feminist assertion and exploration in Germany. In 1887, well-known lesbians and women's rights figures Anita Augspurg (1857–1943) and her then-partner Sophia Goudstikker (1865–1924) had opened their studio, Hofatelier Elvira, in Munich. It was the first company founded by women in Germany. Adelt-Duc would have known of them and may well have met them. Between 1903 and 1914, she traveled extensively and regularly wrote for German photography magazines. Hers were popular pieces focusing on European tourism. Her letters, notes, and articles gave advice on railway connections, popular locale excursions, and suitable cameras. She also offered journalistic snapshots of the life and customs that she encountered in places such as Cairo, Damascus, Djibouti, Addis Ababa, and Harar; Sudan, Arabia, Siam, Burma, Nepal, Tibet, and of course India.

Aside from these pieces, Adelt-Duc published a travel guide, *Südindien und Burma* (*South India and Burma*), for a multilingual series in 1909, and the noteworthy collection *Indische Novellen* (*Indian Novellas*) in 1914. The latter text enabled her to accomplish in her fiction what she had been able only to gesture toward in *Ich will!* and to train her attention on life in colonial India. The collection is simultaneously—and in equal parts—conventional and unconventional. On the one hand, the novellas belong to a familiar genre of colonial writing by non-Indians from British India. Such writing was typically produced by colonial officials or missionaries or their family members, often their wives. Adelt-Duc's stories bear many of the expected characteristics of such prose: a bewildered European gaze cast upon the colonial subject, the native "other"; a preoccupation with themes such as romantic love or spirituality; an often exoticizing and orientalist depiction of what European readers might then have proceeded to perceive as a so-called authentic narrative concerning the East. On the other hand, Adelt-Duc's novellas, like her earlier fiction, provide multiple representations of strong, unconventional female protagonists: a female fraudster and marriage swindler who proposes a faux marriage for her own advantage and Indians and non-Indians engaged in forbidden interracial love. Readers even encounter a cross-dressing male protagonist, whose masquerade results in a homosexual kiss—a provocative and subversive scene for the time and context. Often offering a sharp criticism of the colonial lifestyle, the collection testifies to

Adelt-Duc's intimate familiarity with the customs and traditions of colonial India.

Little is known of Adelt-Duc after the start of World War I, which seems to have all but ended her career. It is also not known whether, or when, she would have learned of her daughter's marriage in 1915, the birth of a grandson in 1917, or her daughter's death in 1918. In 1926, she and Riebeling returned to a Germany—and a Europe—that had undergone significant cultural and political change. The feminist and lesbian cultures of the Weimar Republic were markedly different from those of imperial Germany at the start of the century. Some of the goals for which the women's movement had fought in the latter half of the nineteenth century had been achieved. Women could attend university and they could vote. Middle-class women's professional opportunities had expanded; women were able to practice law. Moreover, Berlin, where Adelt-Duc had spent much of her twenties and early thirties, had become a vibrant European center for gay and lesbian life. In addition to the private gatherings that had been in place for decades, by the 1920s there were lesbian bars and cabarets and a dynamic literary scene. There were also lesbian sports clubs, outgrowths of more covert and informally organized clubs available at the turn of the century, such as the cycling group that Minotschka joins in *Are They Women?* It is not known how Adelt-Duc at 60 positioned herself vis-à-vis these new opportunities. In fact, information about her ends in 1930 with the official termination of her marriage to Riebeling, who later, in 1932, returned to the ministry and joined the Nazi Party. Interestingly, the regional records for Lutheran pastors in Germany, which list Riebeling as having been married to "Aimée Duc, writer," designate her as the guilty party in the divorce. Given that under that pseudonym she was and remains best known for her lesbian novel, reissued at some point between 1904 and 1912, it seems likely that the use of the pen name here was a not-so-subtle suggestion of the nature of Adelt-Duc's guilt. We have been unable to find any further record of her.

Are They Women? and the Nineteenth-Century Women's Rights Movement in Germany

The gaps in her biography notwithstanding, Adelt-Duc was clearly quite familiar with the central issues of the women's rights movement in mid- to late-nineteenth-century Germany. Her writings—*Are They Women?* especially—reflect this knowledge.

Three issues to which she returned time and again—education, professional opportunities, and marriage reform—were in fact the three key issues of the women's movement.

Germany's mid- to late-nineteenth-century women's movement was essentially a middle-class movement. It had its roots in the discussions of women's rights that took place in response to the revolutions of 1848, with their calls for liberal changes. In 1849, Louise Otto (or Otto-Peters; 1819–95) founded the *Frauenzeitung* (*Women's Newspaper*), an eight-page weekly paper that, in its brief run from April 1849 until late June 1852, adopted a moderate tone and advocated for women's access to secondary and university education and middle-class professions. Just over a decade later, in 1855, Otto founded the journal *Neue Bahnen* (*New Paths*). In 1865 that publication became the official organ for the Allgemeiner Deutscher Frauenverein (General German Women's Association), which Otto co-founded with others, including Auguste Schmidt (1833–1902).

In the mid-1860s, German middle-class single women's work opportunities were limited. Women could become governesses or schoolteachers. The Allgemeiner Deutscher Frauenverein sought to increase women's educational and professional possibilities—and not simply in response to women's need to support themselves financially. Reformers stressed the importance of self-cultivation. Women's *Bildung* (or, stated in different terms, in the language of the late-nineteenth-century women's movement, women's right to a "free personality") would benefit women, their families, and the state. Girls' secondary education lagged far behind boys', and girls could not attend German universities. (Indeed, university admission was essentially restricted to economically privileged men.) When in 1867 the University of Zurich in Switzerland granted women admission and women from across Europe began enrolling, the push for German women's higher education gained momentum. In addition to Otto, another activist who worked on this issue was Hedwig Dohm (1831–1919); so, too, in the last decade and a half of the century, did Helene Lange (1848–1930) and the far more progressive Hedwig Kettler (1851–1937) and Minna Cauer (1841–1922). In their advocacy, reformers initially adopted two distinct positions with regard to university access. As Patricia M. Mazón has explained, "Dohm argued for women's admission to all subjects as a basic human right, while Otto made a case for female physicians and teachers, professions for which women were considered naturally suited and which would benefit society" (*Gender* 53–54). While one can see both positions in play in *Are They Women?*—most of the third-sex characters are either doctors or medical students; Minotschka, though, has studied a variety of subjects—it is Otto's standpoint that, later taken up by Lange, proved more politically pragmatic in the short and medium term. One might say that Otto and others adapted for their purposes the widespread social and medical view that women were not capable of rigorous study; they argued that access to such study was precisely necessary if women were to fulfill their gender destiny. (In *Are They Women?* Adelt-Duc offers a variation on this debate: she aligns with Italian physician Cesare Lombroso [1835–1909] the position that women are constitutionally unable to engage in intellectual work, and with Krafft-Ebing the counter-argument that women who lack an active intellectual life are the ones most likely to suffer from hysteria.) So, for example, *Neue Bahnen* successfully linked the issue of women's university admission to questions of health and morality: women doctors, especially those trained as gynecologists, could meet the needs of women reluctant to discuss their health concerns with male doctors.

In terms of university study, few gains were made in the 1870s and 1880s. Even so, the issue remained a primary focus of the Allgemeiner Deutscher Frauenverein, which provided German women with scholarships to attend Swiss universities. At the same time, reformers succeeded in developing more possibilities for girls' secondary education. In 1889 in Berlin, Lange and Cauer, along with Franziska Tiburtius (1843–1927), who had studied medicine at the University of Zurich and who had opened her own private practice, established the first high school with the express mission of preparing girls for university. State by state, between 1900 and 1909, German universities granted women admission.

While the German women's movement may have favored "an ideology of 'difference,'" as Mazón states (*Gender* 53), individual leaders such as Cauer, Augspurg, and Marie Stritt (1855–1928) represented the movement's radical wing, promoting the rights of women on the basis of gender equality. Cauer, who in 1888 had founded Frauenwohl (the Women's Welfare Association) and in 1893 cofounded the Mädchen- und Frauengruppen für Soziale Hilfsarbeit (Girls and Women's Groups for Social Assistance Work), joined with Augspurg and Stritt in 1894 and formed the Bund Deutscher Frauenvereine (Federation of German Women's Associations). Composed of middle- and upper-class women from across the liberal and conservative political spectra, the Bund campaigned for women's education, professional opportunities, and rights regarding marriage and divorce. In 1896, Cauer served as president of Der Internationale Kongress für Frauenwerke und Frauenbestrebungen (International Congress of Women's Work and Endeavors), in which both Augspurg and Stritt also played prominent roles. The conference, held in Berlin, was the first of its kind; it is possible that Adelt-Duc would have attended.

That same year, Augspurg became head of the newly formed Verein für Frauen-Studium (Association for Women's University Study) in Berlin and, along with revolutionary socialist Rosa Luxemburg (1871–1919), co-founded the Internationaler Studentinnenverein (International Female Students Association). A year later, she obtained her law degree from the University of Zurich. While women were unable to practice law in Germany until 1922, Augspurg nonetheless was able to provide women with legal advice. She also drew on her training to call for marriage reform. Her 1905 "Ein typischer Fall der Gegenwart. Ein offener Brief" ("A Typical Case of the Present Time. An Open Letter"), which enumerates the various ways in which marriage disempowered women and presents free union as an alternative to marriage that enabled women to safeguard their independence and individuality, proves a powerful example of her feminist analysis (see Appendix B1).

Stritt held many of these same views. Like Augspurg, she promoted marriage reform. Additionally, she called for family planning (including the use of contraception and access to safe abortions) and together with Augspurg sought to protect the rights of prostitutes. The two women, along with Augspurg's partner Lida Gustava Heymann (1868–1943), whom Augspurg had met at the 1896 Congress and with whom she founded the Verein für Frauenstimmrecht (German Association for Women's Suffrage) in 1902, also worked on behalf of women's right to vote.

Late-Nineteenth-Century Sexology

With its emphasis on educational access, professional opportunities, marriage reform, and birth control, the late-nineteenth-century German women's movement proved important for lesbians, for whom the issue of leading lives apart from men held heightened significance. Yet even as some of the movement's leaders were lesbian (as were Augspurg and, arguably, Cauer), lesbian recognition and acceptance were not part of the movement's platform.

Discussions of lesbianism did occur in medical texts, such as *Psychopathia Sexualis* by Krafft-Ebing, *Die Conträre Sexualempfindung* (*Contrary Sexual Instinct*) by Albert Moll (1862–1939), and *Sexual Inversion* by Havelock Ellis (1859–1939) and John Addington Symonds (1840–93). Although Moll's offered the most attention to lesbianism, all of these textbooks focused primarily on male homosexuality. The first study to concentrate on women and homosexuality, *Der Konträrsexualismus inbezug auf Ehe und Frauenfrage* (*Contrary-Sexuality in Relation to Marriage and the Woman Question*), was written by a woman who was not a doctor, Emma Trosse (1863–1949). The first journal devoted to issues of sexual and gender minorities, the *Yearbook for Intermediate Sexual Types*, was founded in 1899 by Magnus Hirschfeld. These works built on a mid-century Austro-German tradition of inquiry into same-sex attraction, personified by such figures as early homosexual rights advocate Karl Heinrich Ulrichs (1825–95), who coined the term "Urning" (or "Uranian");[1] Austro-Hungarian journalist Károly Mária Kertbeny (1824–82), who is credited with the first use of the term "homosexual" in 1869;[2] and Berlin-born psychiatrist Karl Friedrich Otto Westphal (1833–90), who introduced the term "contrary sexual instinct" (sometimes translated as "contrary sexual feeling") in that same year.[3]

Of these works, *Psychopathia Sexualis* and *Sexual Inversion* have proven to be the most influential. First published in 1886 and subsequently revised and expanded, *Psychopathia Sexualis* contained a number of case studies, a few of which focused on homosexual women and some of which later appeared in the works of his contemporaries. Initially presenting same-sex behavior as a perversion to be condemned, Krafft-Ebing came to modify his position and to call for tolerance for homosexuals.

Moll, who edited the 1924 edition of *Psychopathia Sexualis*, saw his own *Die Conträre Sexualempfindung* published in 1891. Unlike his contemporaries, including Sigmund Freud (1856–

---

1 For Urning, see Ulrichs 50. Following Ulrichs, British poet, literary critic, and homosexual rights advocate John Addington Symonds, who would meet Ulrichs in 1891, used the term "Uranian" in *A Problem in Greek Ethics* 43. Symonds's work is reprinted as Appendix A in Ellis and J.A. Symonds. The reference to "uranian love" appears on p. 203.

2 For Kertbeny's coining of "homosexual," see Weeks 16.

3 See also Ellis and Symonds 27.

1939), whose well-known essay "Die sexuellen Abirrungen" ("The Sexual Aberrations") appeared as part of his *Drei Abhandlungen zur Sexualtheorie* (*Three Essays on the Theory of Sexuality*) in 1905, Moll was not interested in whether homosexuality was either inherited or acquired. He argued that homosexuality was a tendency innate in all heterosexuals, as was heterosexuality in all homosexuals. Moll advocated the decriminalization of homosexuality even as he regarded it as a pathology that in adults required treatment. In contrast to Freud, who in his essay justifies his lack of attention to women because of "their conventional secretiveness and insincerity" (17), Moll devotes his text's final chapter, some 80 pages long, to a discussion of the contrary sexual instinct in women.

In comparison to Moll's understanding of sexual variation, the position of England's foremost sexologist, Havelock Ellis, was more sympathetic. Like Moll, he did not regard homosexuality as a crime; unlike him, however, he did not think that inversion (his preferred term for homosexuality) was a disease. His major work, *Sexual Inversion*, initially published in German in 1896 and then in English in 1897, includes a chapter on women that did much to reify the stereotype of the ugly lesbian (see Appendix D1). Here, he distinguishes between two types of homosexuals: on the one hand, "[a] class of women ... [whose] homosexuality, while fairly distinct, is only slightly marked ... the pick of the women whom the average man would pass by," and, on the other hand, "actively inverted" women, characterized by "a more or less distinct trace of masculinity ... [which is] part of an organic instinct" (p. 127). It is also important to recognize that in that chapter, as in the text as a whole, Ellis's discussion of homosexuality and homosexuals occurred alongside his avowal of a racial hierarchy. For him, as for other sexologists and women's rights activists including Augspurg, attention to same-sex behaviors across cultures served as a means to affirm the racial superiority of people of European descent.

For his part, sexologist Magnus Hirschfeld, who in 1897 cofounded the Wissenschaftlich-humanitäres Komitee (hereafter Scientific-Humanitarian Committee), oversaw that organization's publication, the *Yearbook for Intermediate Sexual Types*, whose first volume appeared in 1899. Differentiating among gender and sexual categories to a greater degree than his contemporaries, he was an early researcher in transgender studies (in which work he was followed by Ellis). Hirschfeld popularized terms such as intermediate sexual types, the third sex, transvestite, and transsexual. The most politically engaged of the sexologists, he was Germany's outspoken champion for gender and sexual minorities, and later, in 1919, in Berlin, he opened the Institut für Sexualwissenschaft (Institute of Sexology), the first of its kind. Together with the Committee, Hirschfeld fought for gender and sexual minorities' recognition and against their legal persecution. To this end, the *Yearbook* served as a means of education, outreach, and advocacy, including for lesbian reformers such as Anna Rüling (pseudonym of Theodora "Theo" Anna Sprüngli; 1880–1953), and each edition included a list of relevant national and international publications, scientific, sociological, and literary. Even so, the reviewer of *Are They Women?* in the *Yearbook*'s 1903 volume remained impervious to the novel's significance for lesbian literary representation.

In contrast to Hirschfeld and the others discussed thus far, Emma Trosse was not a sexologist. Nor are her writings, strictly speaking, scientific. Still, her contribution to the study of women and contrary sexuality should not be overlooked. Drawing on literature, history, and science, her 1895 pamphlet *Der Konträrsexualismus* advanced the first full-length argument to focus on lesbianism. It was followed two years later by *Ein Weib? Psychologisch-biographische Studie über eine Konträrsexuelle (A Woman? Psychological-Biographical Study Concerning a Contrary-Sexual Woman)*, whose questioning title, like that of Adelt-Duc's novel, encodes the gender instability that lesbianism occasions. A teacher and a poet, Trosse had wide-ranging interests, literary as well as scientific. Beginning with her 1895 pamphlet, she argued for the acceptance of homosexuals, the acknowledgement of their fundamental humanity, and the recognition of their contributions to the social good. In so doing, she led the way for other writers interested in exploring the intersection of lesbianism and women's rights.

Essays on Women's Rights and Lesbian Recognition at the Turn of the Nineteenth Century

While, apart from Trosse's work, late-nineteenth-century texts engaging sexology failed to give lesbianism substantial attention, contemporary German women's rights publications, whether or not they invoked scientific arguments, offered little better. Only a few mentioned, let alone discussed, lesbian desire. *Are They Women?* is one of those exceptions. Three others are as follows: from 1897, *Noli me tangere! Dunkle Punkte aus dem modernen*

Frauenleben (Noli me tangere! Dark Spots in the Modern Life of Women); from 1903, *Was hat der Mann aus Weib, Kind und sich gemacht? Revolution und Erlösung des Weibes. Eine Abrechnung mit dem Mann—Ein Wegweiser in die Zukunft! (What Has Man Made of Woman, Child and Himself? Woman's Revolution and Salvation. Settling Up with the Man—A Guide into the Future)*, by Johanna Elberskirchen (1864–1943); and from 1904, the powerful speech "Welches Interesse hat die Frauenbewegung an der Lösung der homosexuellen Problems?," (hereafter "What Interest Does the Women's Movement Have in Solving the Homosexual Problem?"), delivered by journalist Anna Rüling.

Noli me tangere![1] was one of the first German writings to address lesbianism within the context of women's rights. The author, presumably a woman, is not known. The text was published in Leipzig by Max Spohr (1850–1905) in the same year that he, together with Hirschfeld and others, founded the Scientific-Humanitarian Committee. Given both Spohr's association with Hirschfeld and his specialized publishing in this area from 1893 forward, *Noli me tangere!* would have enjoyed instant visibility and credibility.

Well written and convincingly argued, the text focuses primarily on the need for marriage reform, which it frames as both a feminist and a lesbian issue. With regard to the latter, it is important to recognize that in contrast to male homosexuality, which was criminalized under the infamous Paragraph 175 of the German Criminal Code, lesbianism was not. Indeed, a subsequent attempt in 1907 to render it punishable was defeated in the German Parliament when legislators foundered on defining female sexuality. By contrast, in late-nineteenth-century Austria, both male and female homosexual activity were criminalized. Yet, as Krafft-Ebing notes in *Psychopathia Sexualis*, no Austrian court had ever charged a woman with a homosexual offence. The view that women were naturally less sensual than men remained dominant in both countries. Because of that understanding of women's sexuality, as Krafft-Ebing observed, "inverted sexual intercourse among women [was] less noticeable and, ... [often] considered mere friendship."[2] Women's sexuality was regarded primarily through the lens of marriage. With her marriage critique, the author of *Noli me tangere!* in effect

---

1   Latin: "touch me not."
2   Krafft-Ebing, *Psychopathia Sexualis*, 12th ed., pp. 395–96.

found an effective means of making lesbianism legible to her readership.

Noli me tangere! lays out four demands for the improvement of married women's lives. First, women needed to be able to retain their freedom and independence within marriage. Legal union was to support, not diminish, women's rights. Second, there needed to be a sensible reduction in the number of children. Women had to be given reproductive choice, since they bore the children and served as their primary caretakers. Third, marriage needed to be recognized primarily as a comradeship between two individuals who had come together not in order to lose but rather to nourish their individuality. Finally, divorce had to be made more easily obtainable and its proceedings less complicated.

Having articulated these demands, *Noli me tangere!*'s author then directs her attention to married lesbians. As turn-of-the-century Germany did not offer women many social and economic alternatives to marriage, she explains, many women who were not at all suited for marriage had been forced into it. Anticipating the formulations of the third sex at work in *Are They Women?*, she states, "it is the best of women who do not wish to marry" (8). In what is perhaps one of the earliest references to the 1-in-10 statistic, she remarks that some 10% of women were "women with contrary sexual instincts" (14, 17). "A part of nature" (14), they would never want to marry or have children. Yet the lack of viable alternatives in effect obliged such women to do both. The author cited her own familiarity with informal gatherings of lesbians in each other's homes in Berlin and Munich. These meetings provided occasions for forming both friendships and intimacies; many of those women present, she noted, were married. The implicitly posed question here was whether marriage's erasure of women in effect produced lesbian possibility: that is, within *Noli me tangere!*'s analysis, lesbianism functions as both a symptom of and solution to marriage's failure of women. Given that failure, all women, as well as men, would benefit from relationships based on free love, rather than economic or legal necessity.

Whereas the author of *Noli me tangere!* addresses lesbianism's significance for the women's movement, Anna Rüling foregrounds it. Her essay, which she delivered as a speech to the Scientific-Humanitarian Committee in 1904, was later published in its *Yearbook* in 1905 (see Appendix C1 for a translation of the full text). It is a powerful early-twentieth-century German articulation of the relationship between lesbian advocacy and women's rights, and of the three essays the one most closely related to *Are They Women?* For Rüling, any critical examination of marriage reform needed to acknowledge lesbianism. Presenting a broad definition of lesbian, she explained that there were not simply "normal" women but also "vastly differing gradations in the transition between the sexes": there were both "absolute" and "merely psychological" lesbians (Appendix C1, p. 111). The former were women who were sexually attracted to women and were characterized by their "clear-eyed reason" (p. 111). Absolute lesbians did not imitate men; instead, they were of men's "predisposition" (p. 111). Psychological lesbians, too, were marked by their mental energy and objectivity, but their sex drive, she argues, was either not particularly strong or inclined them toward "feminine" men (p. 111). More than 75 years before Adrienne Rich (1929–2012) in her 1980 essay "Compulsory Heterosexuality and Lesbian Existence,"[1] Rüling, building on Hirschfeld's work, put forward her formulation of a lesbian continuum. Given Germany's surplus of women, the relationships that both absolute and psychological lesbians held toward marriage necessarily affected so-called heterosexual women, the majority of whom, Rüling reassured her audience, followed traditional gender norms; they fulfilled their destiny as wives and mothers. Freeing those women whose nature compelled them to find fulfilment in other spheres—possibly some heterosexual women but certainly many lesbians—so that they might pursue educational and professional opportunities would in turn not only enable them to find means of supporting themselves apart from marriage but also increase the chances of women who were "organically determined ... to be a wife and mother" (p. 116) to find husbands.

---

1 In her essay, Rich defines "lesbianism" capaciously in order to simultaneously destigmatize the term and underscore the primary affective bonds of women across sexual identity categories. Rüling makes a similar rhetorical move. Her discussion of "absolute" and "psychological" lesbians may recall the distinctions made by some of her contemporaries, who considered the varying degrees of inversion in women (see, for example, Havelock Ellis in Appendix D1). Yet Rüling's argument differs from theirs in so far as she, like Rich, identifies various types of lesbianism in order to stress the commonalities between women and, by extension, their shared investment in women's rights.

Providing lesbians with alternatives to marriage would benefit not only heterosexual women but also men, future generations, and ultimately the state. Men who married lesbians would be able to find neither personal happiness nor sexual satisfaction; they would be cheated of both. Nor would they likely produce healthy offspring. In a line of reasoning reminiscent of Krafft-Ebing's linkage of homosexuality to congenital illnesses, Rüling argued that expanding women's possibilities for earning their livelihoods and so reducing the number of lesbians resigned to marriage was a matter of national well-being: "[E]xperience teaches us that the progeny of Uranians is only in the rarest of cases healthy and strong. The unhappy creatures, conceived without love, even without desire, constitute a large percentage of the feebleminded, idiots, epileptics, consumptives, *degenerates* of all sorts" (p. 113; emphasis in original).

Nor would increased educational and professional possibilities for women prove disadvantageous. Men would benefit, since for the "vast majority" of heterosexual women, access to a more rounded education would allow them to become companions "equal to" their husbands. Lesbians, in turn, given their "greater objectivity, capability, and stamina," would be ideally suited to become doctors and lawyers, and in those roles they would strengthen society (p. 117).

In sum, it was the duty of the women's movement to support not only women's rights but also lesbians' rights. The struggle for women's personal liberation and lesbians' struggle for the right to love were necessarily intertwined.

For her part, Johanna Elberskirchen took issue with the prominence that female masculinity held in arguments such as Rüling's regarding lesbianism and the women's movement. For Elberskirchen, a sexologist who, trained in law as well as medicine, was herself an active member of the Scientific-Humanitarian Committee, homosexual exceptionalism existed, but it was not, in the case of lesbians or lesbian members of the women's movement, vitally linked to masculinity. As she stressed in her pamphlet *Die Liebe des dritten Geschlechts* (*Love among the Third Sex*), published by Max Spohr later in 1904, homosexuals were not shameful or degenerate, and their love, in contrast to marriage, which had brought such suffering on women, was of a higher order. Because they were not burdened by the drive to reproduce, homosexuals could serve society both intellectually and spiritually. One needed, though, to understand homosexuality apart from gender inversion. For example, lesbianism, as she maintained in *Was hat der Mann aus Weib, Kind und sich gemacht?*, entailed a turn toward the feminine: women desiring each other. Nor was the women's movement, in advocating the expansion of women's educational and professional opportunities, seeking to masculinize women. The movement was rather a struggle against male domination. There were no essential differences between men and women, she argued. Male oppression had made women inferior. Emancipation would allow women to realize their physical and intellectual potential, and, ultimately, the differences between men and women would disappear. Deft in its reasoning and often tongue-in-cheek in its tone, Elberskirchen's work, like Rüling's, anticipates German lesbian and feminist debates later in the century.

The Emergence of Lesbian Literature at the Turn of the Nineteenth Century

Of the German lesbian writings published at the turn of the century, none better captures the discussions at the intersection of women's rights and the third sex than *Are They Women?* Yet, as much as Adelt-Duc was invoking contemporary lesbian and feminist arguments, she was also responding to an emerging literary interest in the exploration of lesbian life. Some of the texts that were part of this effort are as follows: *Der Liebe Lust und Leid der Frau zur Frau* (*Desire and Sorrow in the Love between Woman to Woman* [1895]), attributed to Emilie Knopf; the "Lulu" plays, *Erdgeist* (*Earth Spirit* [1895]) and *Die Büchse der Pandora* (*Pandora's Box* [1902]) by Frank Wedekind (1864–1918); *Das dritte Geschlecht* (*The Third Sex* [1899]) by Ernst von Wolzogen; *Auf Kypros* (*On Cyprus* [1900]) by Baroness Gertrud von Puttkamer (1881–1941); *Dr. Erna Redens Thorheit und Erkenntnis* (*Dr. Erna Reden's Foolishness and Insight* [1900]) by Alfred Meebold (1863–1952); *Vom neuen Weibe und seiner Liebe. Ein Buch für reife Geister* (*On the New Woman and Her Love. A Book for Mature Minds* [1900]) by Elisabeth Dauthendey (1854–1943); *Zwei Frauen* (*Two Women* [1901]) by August Niemann (1839–1919); *Das vierte Geschlecht* (*The Fourth Sex* [1901]) by Valeska Hoffmann; *Die neue Eva* (*The New Eve* [1902]) by Maria Janitschek (1859–1927); and *Auf Vorposten. Roman aus meiner Züricher Studienzeit* (*On the Outpost Watch: Novel of My Student Days in Zurich* [1903]) by Ella Mensch (1859–1935).

Writing into a cultural context that viewed lesbianism as a phase, a pathology, or a crime, *fin-de-siècle* authors were necessarily pressured to relegate lesbian characters to minor, tragic, or vilifying roles. Very few texts accorded lesbian stories serious or positive attention. So, for example, in Wedekind's acclaimed plays *Erdgeist* and *Die Büchse der Pandora*, the lesbian character Gräfin (Countess) Geschwitz, while a sympathetic figure, is nonetheless tragically killed when she attempts to prevent the murder of the woman she loves. Similarly, both Meebold's novella *Dr. Erna Redens Thorheit und Erkenntniss* and Janitschek's novella collection *Die neue Eva* cast lesbian attraction as dangerous.

Same-sex eroticism also receives coded, passing attention in *Auf Vorposten*. With this novel, Mensch, who was a conservative member of the women's movement and one of the first German women to receive a doctorate in literature from the University of Zurich, drew on her own experiences of the student milieu. Her protagonist recalls the self-reliant, intellectually serious, and gender-transgressive characters of *Are They Women?* The homoeroticism in play in Mensch's novel is absent from her later, non-literary work, *Bilderstürmer der Berliner Frauenbewegung (Iconoclasts of Berlin's Women's Movement)*. Itself a response to Wilhelm Hammer's study with the prurient title *Die Tribadie Berlins (Tribadism in Berlin* [1906]), Mensch's book dismissed the idea that lesbians could play a prominent role in the women's movement. Lesbians, she argued, were intrinsically passive and withdrawn outsiders, necessarily out of touch with the concerns of normal women.

In a handful of texts, lesbian love proves a prominent issue. One example, notable for its favorable rendering, is the collection of lyric poems *Auf Kypros (On Cyprus)*, written by Puttkamer under the pseudonym Marie-Madeleine. Over the next four decades, *Auf Kypros* sold over one million copies. *Der Liebe Lust und Leid* is, for its part, thought to be the first lesbian novel in German. Explicit descriptions of erotic encounters and the sensuality of female physical beauty distinguish this novel, which starts—and abruptly ends—with a disillusioned renunciation of lesbian love as mental confusion and immoral behavior. This narrative frame might well signal an authorial attempt to avoid censorship. The anonymously published novel may have been written by one Emilie Knopf, who was named as the author in a court proceeding in which she and a friend were fined for distributing obscene material (see Dobler). Aside from a newspaper account of the event, nothing more is known of Knopf. Dauthendey's novel *Vom neuen Weibe und seiner Liebe* in turn examines passionate female friendship, even as it condemns explicitly sexual lesbian relationships. Importantly, her "Die Urnische Frage und die Frau" ("The Uranian Question and Woman" [1906]) indicates a moderation in her position. Published in the *Yearbook for Intermediate Sexual Types*, the essay advocated that lesbians be understood as distinct from normal women and regarded with consideration. Finally, Niemann's novel *Zwei Frauen*, which explicitly references Wolzogen's, portrays a married woman's love affair with a female colleague who is a member of the "third sex." The outcome is necessarily negative: the third sex seductress disappears, while the wife goes mad and dies a slow and sorrowful death.

Of all the novels that preceded Adelt-Duc's *Are They Women?*, Wolzogen's *Das dritte Geschlecht* proved to be the most successful. In a strict sense, it is not a lesbian work at all: written by a man, it is a satirical take on the gender-troubling New Woman. One of the characters in the novel recalls the openly lesbian women's rights leader Anita Augspurg, a figure whom Wolzogen continued to caricature in other writings.

Like Adelt-Duc's text, *Das vierte Geschlecht* answers Wolzogen. Hoffmann's novel proves a witty response, focusing on a group of employed, independent women, that is, members of the third sex. Outraged by Wolzogen's disparaging attitude, they invent the term "the fourth sex" in order to describe men who, like Wolzogen, disrespect women (see Schmersahl 190).

Read against this literary history, Adelt-Duc's *Are They Women?*, with its affirming representations of lesbians and its happy ending, is truly pioneering. Indeed, the text's positive view lays the groundwork for better known and aesthetically engaging examples of lesbian literature from the Weimar Period (1919–33), such as the erotically charged trilogy *Der Skorpion* (*The Scorpion* [1919, 1920, 1931]) by Anna Elisabet Weirauch (1887–1970) and the poignantly compelling play by Christa Winsloe (1888–1944), *Ritter Nérestan* (*Knight Nérestan* [1930]), also called *Gestern und Heute* (*Yesterday and Today*). The play was made into the lesbian film classic *Mädchen in Uniform* (*Girls in Uniform* [1931]) and recast as the bestselling novel *Das Mädchen Manuela* (*The Girl Named Manuela* [1933]). Produced within the context of the era's rich artistic and cultural flowering, these texts reflect the expanded possibilities for personal expression that, in particular for lesbians and gay men, were unavailable at the beginning of the century. The lesbian writings of that earlier period are all but forgotten. We hope that our translation and critical edition of *Are They Women?* have laid the foundation for further research on that body of literature which Adelt-Duc helped define.

Mina Adelt-Duc: A Brief Chronology

1867   Born Hedwig Maria Mina Adelt in Breslau on 1 May.
        Father: postal official Ferdinand (Eduard Ferdinand
        Wilhelm) Adelt (1828–91); mother: Elisa Duc
        (1832–1902). Siblings: Adeline (1862–?) and Eduard
        Ferdinand (1876–?). From 1873, raised and educated
        in Strasbourg. Later known as Mina (or Minna)
        Wettstein-Adelt and then Mina Adelt-Duc. Pseudo-
        nyms: Aimée Duc, Helvetia (attributed)

1889   Marriage on 23 March in Rorschach, Switzerland, to
        Oskar (Markus Oskar) Wettstein (1866–1952), a
        Swiss journalist, later editor-in-chief of the *Züricher
        Post*

1889   Birth of daughter, Maria Marta Aimée, on 21 August
        in Jena, Germany

1890   Move to Berlin. Member of the German women's
        movement

1891   *Des Hauses Tausendkünstler. Ein treuer Rathgeber für den
        Haushalt* [*The Household Wizard. A Faithful Guide for
        the Household*], pamphlet

1892   "Körperliche Übungen für Mädchen" ["Physical
        Exercises for Girls"], in *Blatt der Hausfrau* [*Home-
        maker's Newspaper*]

1892   "Hauswirtschaftlicher Unterricht" ["Lessons in Home
        Economics"], in *Blatt der Hausfrau*

1893   *3½ Monate Fabrik-Arbeiterin* [*Female Factory Worker for
        3½ Months*]

1893   *Macht euch frei! Ein Wort an die deutschen Frauen* [*Free
        Yourselves! A Word to German Women*], pamphlet

1893   "Zur Arbeiterinnenfrage" ["On the Question of
        Female Factory Workers"], in *Ethische Kultur* [*Ethical
        Culture*]

1893   "Die Putzsucht der Arbeiterin" ["The Working-Class
        Woman's Addiction to Cleaning"], in *Ethische Kultur*

1893   "Zur Fürsorge für unbemittelte Frauen und
        Mädchen" ["On the Care of Indigent Women and
        Girls"], in *Blätter für soziale Praxis in Gemeinde, Vere-
        inen und Privatleben* [*Papers on Social Praxis in Commu-
        nities, Organisations, and Private Life*]

1893   "Am Wege" ["By the Roadside"] and "Das Spinnen"
        ["Spinning"], in *Blatt der Hausfrau*
1893   "Das Erwerbsleben der Frau" ["The Woman's Life as
        an Employee"], in *Ethische Kultur*
1893   "Der Frauentag in Wiesbaden, 5.–7. Juni" ["Women's
        Day in Wiesbaden, 5–7 June"], in *Ethische Kultur*
1893–   Editor of *Berliner Modenkorrespondenz* [*Berlin Fashion*
1900   *Correspondence*]
1894   "Der Muff" ["The Muff"], *Blatt der Hausfrau*
1894   "Erzählung einer Radfahrerin" ["Tale of a Female
        Cyclist"], in *Berliner Börsencourier* [*Stock Exchange
        Courier*]
1894   Editor of *Für die Frau. Organ für die Interessen der
        Frauenwelt in Stadt und Land* [*For Women. A Voice for
        Women's Interests in Town and Country*], a quarterly
        magazine
1894   *Im dunkelsten Berlin* [*In Darkest Berlin*]. Advertised but
        not published; was to be published by J. Leiser in
        Berlin
1894   "Sommerreisen alleinstehender Frauen" ["Single
        Women's Summer Travels"], *Blatt der Hausfrau*
1894   Chair of Berlin's newly founded Damen-Radfahr-
        Verein [Women's Cycling Association]; named in
        December
1895–99 Founding editor-in-chief of *Draisena. Blätter für
        Damenradfahren. Organ zur Pflege und Förderung des
        Radfahrens der Damen* [*Draisena. Newspaper for Women's
        Cycling. Voice for the Support and Promotion of Women's
        Cycling*]; in subsequent years the title reads *Draisena.
        Erstes und ältestes Sportblatt der radfahrenden Damen*
        [*Draisena. First and Oldest Sports Newspaper for Women
        Cyclists*]. Published biweekly in Dresden and in
        Vienna. The last issue appeared in January 1900
1895   "Kinder als Straßenverkäufer" ["Children as
        Streetvendors"], *Hamburgische Schulzeitung* [*The
        Hamburg School Paper*]
1895   "Dienstboten im Lande" ["Servants in the Country"],
        Blatt der Hausfrau
1896   "Unsere Stimmmittel" ["Our Means for Voting"],
        Blatt der Hausfrau
1896   "Eine winterliche Segelfahrt" ["A Wintry Sailing
        Trip"], *Pester Lloyd*

1896	Divorce from Wettstein, finalized 17 December. Daughter remains with Wettstein
1897	"Das sportliche Leben der Schwedin" ["The Swedish Woman's Sporty Life"], *Sport im Bild* [*Sports in Pictures*]
1898	*Berliner Haushaltungsschulen*" ["Berlin Schools for Home Economics"], *Für Alle Welt* [*For All the World*]
1900	Attendee, IXe Congrès Universel de la Paix [9th Universal Peace Congress] in Paris, 30 September–5 October
1901	*Sind es Frauen? Roman über das dritte Geschlecht* [*Are They Women? A Novel Concerning the Third Sex*]
1901	Civil marriage to Lutheran pastor Theodor Konrad Riebeling (1870–1959), 14 September in Birmingham, England
1901	"Der Sport als ethischer Faktor" ["Sport as an Ethical Consideration"], *Ethische Kultur*
1901	"Die englische Bühne" ["The English Stage"], in *Das neue Jahrhundert* [*The New Century*]
1902	"Die Temperenzfrage in England" ["The Temperance Issue in England"], in *Ethische Kultur*
1902	"Zur Ethik der Kindheit" ["On the Ethics of Childhood"], *Ethische Kultur*
1902	*Ich will! Freier Wille der Frau und die Folge des Durchsetzens des Willens gegen allen gesellschaftlichen Zwang* [*I Do! Women's Free Will and the Consequences of Meeting Social Coercion with Resolve*]
1902	"Der Thierarzt in Ägypten" ["The Veterinarian in Egypt"], *Berliner Tierärztliches Register* [*Berlin Veterinary Registry*]
1903	Living in Cairo, Egypt
1903	Articles on Greece and Egypt in *Deutsche Photographen-Zeitung* [*The German Photographer's Newspaper*]
1903	"Brief aus Patras" ["Letter from Patras"], *Die Zeit*, 18 August
1904	*Des Pastors Liebe. Ein modernes Sittenbild* [*The Pastor's Love. A Portrait of Modern Manners*]
1904	Founder of the business Asiatisch-Orientalische Industriekorrespondenz [Asiatic-Oriental Industry Correspondence]. Later, the business has offices in Alexandria, Cairo, Damascus, Smyrna, Bombay, Calcutta, Birmingham, and London

1904   Two "Reisebriefe" ["Travel Letters"]; articles "Der
        Juwelier in Ägypten" ["The Jeweler in Egypt"] and
        "Zum Geschäftsverkehr mit Smyrna" ["On Trade
        Relations with Smyrna"], *Deutsche Goldschmiedezeitung*
        [*Newspaper for German Goldsmiths*]
c. 1904 Moves to India
1905   *Die Emmaus-Frage. Auch eine Kritik der reinen Vernunft*
        [*Die Emmaus Question. Also a Critique of Pure Reason*]
1905   "Bombays Wälder" ["Bombay's Forest"], *Deutsche
        Forstzeitung* [*German Paper of Forestry*]
1906   "Löschverhältnisse in Palästina" ["Extinguishing Fires
        in Palestine"], *Feuerwehr-Signale* [*Firefighters' Signals*]
1906–07 "Abessinien als Absatzgebiet für kondensierte Milch
        und Butter" ["Abyssinia as a Market for Condensed
        Milk and Butter"], *Milch-zeitung* [*Milk Newspaper*]
1907–14 Articles on cities, regions, and countries in western
        Asia, North Africa, the Indian subcontinent, and
        mainland southeast Asia; emphasis on travel and
        tourism; some articles on camera equipment and
        genres of photography, *Photographisches Wochenblatt*
        [*Photographic Weekly*]
1909   *Südindien und Burma* [*South India and Burma*]
1914   *Indische Novellen* [*Indian Novellas*]
1915   Daughter Maria Marta Aimée marries Robert Blass in
        Zurich
1917   Birth of grandson, Heinz Blass, 2 June
1918   Death of Maria Marta Aimée, 16 December
1920   "Pharmazeutisches aus Indien" ["Pharmaceuticals
        from India"], *Pharmazeutisches Zentralblatt* [*Pharma-
        ceutical Newspaper*]
1926   Listing in 4 January 1926 issue of *The Times of India*
        of "Th. K. Riebeling Adelt Duc" among the first-class
        passengers of the *SS Pilsna*, which departed Bombay
        for Europe on 1 January 1926. Riebeling takes up
        high-school teaching positions in Kassel, Germany
1930   Divorce from Riebeling. Later German Lutheran
        Church list "Aimée Duc" as the guilty party
1930–? No further references to her

A Note on the Text

Our translation is based on the 1901 first edition of *Sind es Frauen? Roman über das dritte Geschlecht*, published in Berlin by Richard Eckstein. In 1976 the Amazonen Frauenverlag Gabriele Meixner published an exact reprint of the edition. We have left the original spellings of all the names and titles of texts, unless noted otherwise. In the case of the *Yearbook for Intermediate Sexual Types* and the Scientific-Humanitarian Committee, we have, after giving the names in the original German, reverted to the English versions because they are in such wide circulation. We have left specific terms (for example, the French word *perron*), if they were used in English at the turn of the nineteenth century, even if that is no longer the case in the twenty-first century. We have also translated those moments of Viennese dialect in the novel into standard English. In general, we have tried to make our translation accord with the English in use at the time of the novel's publication in 1901. Unless otherwise noted, all other translations within the edition are our own. We have tried to preserve authors' original punctuation throughout, but at times we have intervened for clarity's sake: in some instances we have used semicolons instead of commas, and we have shortened sentences.

Ecksteins Moderne Bibliothek Bd. 4.

Aimé Duc ☙ ☙ ☙
Sind es Frauen?

HANS
STUBENRAUCH

ARE THEY WOMEN?
A NOVEL CONCERNING THE THIRD SEX

College was out. One by one, students began leaving the university building, with the large majority still swarming the corridors. Contrary to her usual habit, Minotschka Fernandoff was among the first few who stepped out onto the street.[1] While in principle she tried never to rush, today she hastened out of the building and hurried down the street as quickly as possible. Some people stopped in their tracks, and looked on curiously as she passed by. Strong and well built, the young woman with her rounded form seemed interesting enough. A youthful, unpretentious boyishness gave the unconscious feminine piquancy and coquettishness of her nature a distinctive stamp. She was wearing a smooth, black, tailored cloth dress, a white stand-up collar, a gentleman's necktie and wide cuffs. Sitting casually on her thick, curly hair was a man's plain straw boater. She carried gloves made of substantial, yellow chamois leather in her left hand, and clutched her briefcase under her arm. With her right hand, she leaned on an elegant walking stick, with a large silver handle. The ever-present stick was, at the beginning of her stay in the university town, enough to ensure that everyone would turn around and look at her. Not surmising the actual and very simple reason for this habit, they searched for ugly, dark motives. And yet Minotschka only carried the stick because she could not climb the at-times steep streets of Geneva without effort, and moreover, because of an intermittent nervous weakness affecting her left ankle.

Minotschka Fernandoff did not seem to notice the crowds gawking at her, or, fully aware of her own extraordinary personality, she had long become used to it. With head held high, she always directed her gaze forward. Her step might have been a bit too firm and strong for a woman, but this energetic and yet elastic gait suited her entire appearance. Now she had reached the last house on the street; slowly, as if overcome by sudden fatigue, she climbed the stairs. She unlocked one of the doors facing the landing and entered the room. It was an odd room; though it wasn't small, it overflowed with furniture. At first glance, the numerous framed photographs, the many curtains and runners, the countless bouquets of stunningly fragrant mignonettes and roses were astounding. In the middle of the room stood a table, covered with oval settings, a bit plain in its

---

1   In calling her protagonist Minotschka Fernandoff, Adelt-Duc links
    herself to her character, whose full name offers Russian versions of both
    Mina and Ferdinand, Adelt-Duc's father's name.

decor, yet still pleasing and inviting. On it were large bowls filled with daintily decorated rolls, glass plates with fruits and radishes, cheeses and blood-red tomato salad. Amongst them stood several carafes filled with red and white wine. The student deposited her hat and walking stick in the small bedroom off to the side. Then she washed her hands, sprinkled herself with a penetrating, fragrant perfume and stepped towards the set table. She looked down at it thoughtfully. Suddenly she laughed out-loud and said: "No, it's too bizarre, so her, too! Mais enfin!"[1]

Then, with a careless hand gesture, as if she were throwing something away, she walked over to her desk. She removed a cigarette from a silver case, lit it, and stood still, contemplating the smoke rings floating out the open window. All of a sudden she began whistling the Mimosa Waltz[2] through her teeth, while an odd frivolous smile played on her lips. At that moment, there was a knock on the door. "Entrez!"[3] she called out boldly. "Soyez les bienvenues!"[4] With that she moved toward the door to meet her guests. The two arrivals entered the room and began glancing around. "Hmm, let the feeding of the predators begin!" one of them uttered with a heavy Slavic accent, showing her sparkling white teeth. The other woman, going straight into the bedroom, removed her belongings and observed, "We needn't have hurried, after all; no one else is here yet! But no matter, no harm, it's all the same."[5] Then she passionately embraced the hostess. She was a reasonably pretty girl, though a bit too thin, about twenty-four, and elegantly dressed. Zeline Ardy was a medical student, and as such cared little about her outward appearance. For her, only science was worth taking into consideration. Her companion, Berta Cohn from Prague, was a voluptuous, blond Jewess with an uncommonly good-natured face. She was still quite young, seventeen or eighteen years old. No one could explain why she was already enrolled at

---

1 French: alright already! A subsequent exchange suggests that Minotschka's outburst here signals her discovery of another potential member for her circle of third-sex women.

2 From the musical *The Geisha* (1896) by English composer Sidney Jones (1861–1946).

3 French: come in!

4 French: welcome!

5 In the original version, this last sentence, "But no matter, no harm, it's all the same," is written in Viennese dialect.

the university, but she had passed the requisite entrance exams for foreigners with flying colours. Even so, she was taller, more robust, and stronger than all the others, whom she engaged with maternal condescension. "What a lovely place, Minotschka," she said as she turned to her companion, "though, I dare say, it's a bit small!"

"But that is what I love about it," countered the other, turning away. "Just watch out that you don't knock anything over, you bear cub. I don't want to have to keep telling you 'Buditje ostoroschne!'[1] like the last time at Dreyer's!"[2]

Everyone laughed. Minotschka, whose father was Russian, a Tartar, and whose mother was French, had herself been born in France, and raised as a Frenchwoman. Still, she felt herself to be just as much Russian, and since the students with whom she associated were for the most part either German or Russian, they mixed all the languages together. Even so, they understood each other perfectly.

While they were waiting for the other guests to arrive, their conversation covered any number of topics. The long summer evening was already drawing to a close by the time everyone had arrived and gathered at the table. Frau Annie sat to the left of Minotschka. A pretty thirty-year-old woman, Annie had been married for ten years to a man with whom, after six months, she had reached an agreement. In exchange for half of her villa and a respectable monthly allowance, he would renounce any right to her property. He had consented to this arrangement, and thus these pseudo-spouses continued to live as a married couple. For the sake of their child, whom at the time they were expecting, and who was now nearly ten years of age, they presented themselves as a married couple to the world. Frau Annie single-handedly ran the large institute that she had taken over from her parents. She was a respected, capable, and, for the vast majority of people, a peculiar woman.

To Minotschka's right sat Countess Marta Kinzey, a Polish music student, who, as a millionaire's daughter, was studying only "for her own pleasure." Though fast approaching thirty and certainly not pretty, she was nonetheless thoroughly refined. She occupied an entire floor of a charming villa, and was considered

---

1 Russian: be careful!

2 Here the name Dreyer, homophonically linked to Dreier (or 3er), may well play on the novel's references to the third sex.

to be Minotschka's best friend. In fact, an ardent passion had seized the two of them, and the Polish woman had solely come to Geneva because Minotschka had announced this as her own decision during the winter semester in Leipzig.

Next to the countess sat Zeline, the merry Viennese, then Berta Cohn, and thereafter a French student, Fräulein Dutier, who was joining this circle for the first time that day. A young, lanky thing had taken the seat next to her. Fräulein Hagerbach was German; pale and anemic, she was mockingly dubbed "the Backfish."[1] Completing their group were a second-rate actress from Geneva; a woman from Berlin named Frieda Laube, who was almost as tall as a Prussian guardsman; and Fräulein Dr. Tatjana Kassberg, from Little Russia,[2] currently a resident physician on the gynecological ward of the university hospital. She was a small, nondescript person, with black hair cut short in the Titus style,[3] fiery eyes, and a lively expressive face. A certain cynical, deliberate frivolity in her character made others find her less than likeable. Moreover, no one knew anything about her private relations, though it was tacitly assumed that she was a nihilist. She had a steady flow of male visitors, fellow compatriots. Many of them, though, were in no way members of the university-educated middle class. Moreover, when one of her best friends was recently expelled from Geneva under mysterious circumstances, she did not answer any inquiries, whether made out of interest or curiosity, as to the reasons behind her friend's removal.

The conversation had almost come to a halt. Everybody ate with the healthy appetite of people who worked and were habituated to regular meal times. Only "the Backfish," little Hagerbach from Bavaria, poked at her rolls and confined herself to the sour tomato salad. The wine carafes were being emptied suspi-

---

1 Backfish (or *Backfisch* in German) is an old-fashioned term for a young, adolescent girl or teenager. Common in German through the end of the twentieth century, the term was also used in English around the turn of the nineteenth century. The *Oxford English Dictionary* (*OED*) entry for the term includes examples from American and British texts between 1888 and 1966.

2 "Little Russia" here refers to the geographical territory roughly encompassing Belarus and Ukraine.

3 A short, layered hairstyle, introduced during the French Revolution; as a woman's style, it was criticized for being masculine.

ciously quickly, even though the two Germans and the Polish woman drank almost nothing.

"Stop!" Dr. Kassberg cried suddenly, snatching the tomato salad from the anemic woman. "That is terribly unhealthy for you," she scolded. "You should drink wine instead!" And she poured her a full glass. She spoke an impeccably correct German, with a characteristically harsh Russian inflection.

The Bavarian looked embarrassed, and the Frenchwoman, who had not understood a word, looked at the doctor with surprise.

"My dears," Minotschka exclaimed in the same moment, "my dears, I have to do something mad!"

And in the zeal of emphasising her words, her soft, small boyish hand bent the substantial zinc fork. "Don't be embarrassed," laughed the Viennese woman.

"Yes, but something quite mad!" the first woman insisted again. "Something ..." She stared for a while at her plate and then continued, half-heartedly: "It really was mean of Elise Fritz. Mean."

"Ah, so that's how it is," the Viennese scoffed. "Is it because of her that you are so angry? My goodness, so she was a phony!"[1]

And she continued to eat contentedly.

"But what is one supposed to say then," Minotschka insisted, "when one of us makes it all a lie and slaps us in the face—oh, oh!" The countess responded by lightly placing her hand on Minotschka's arm: "Milaya[2] Minotschka!" she said tenderly in Russian. "Leave it be. We all need to know for ourselves what we are doing. Twice as much so, when we are different from the rest." They spoke Russian together most of the time, and when they were in the company of others, always addressed each other formally. Minotschka did not reply. "Good heavens, what does it matter that Fräulein Fritz got engaged," rasped Dr. Tatjana. "I would do the same thing if it were necessary for my career! Once I have established my own clinic at home, I myself might marry a resident. He would still need to keep his hands to himself and one could love whomever one wanted. Marriage and love are altogether two different matters!"

"But Fritz loves her fiancé," the Jewess explained.

---

1 Sentence originally written in dialect.
2 Russian: sweet.

"Well, yes," the doctor answered in bored fashion. "So she is normal after all, and up until then was mistaken. That's nothing out of the ordinary! Frau Annie, you, my dear Minotschka, and I—we have all been mistaken at times, though in the contrary sense. You both married first, and I, I had a lover—and then we all came to discover that we had no use for a man and belonged to the third sex. With Fritz, it was the other way around!"

Minotschka remained silent. She did not like to hear any mention of her marriage. As a twenty-year old student she had married an upperclassman, her mentor, a young lawyer, only to divorce him three years later. She had not recognised her condition beforehand, and the marriage to the man who loved her more than anything was for her a horror. When after three years she was liberated, she revived. Nowadays she regarded that frightening time, her otherwise pleasant marriage, as a lost time. "A capital investment in happiness," she would often jest when she spoke about it.

"But that is something completely different," she insisted. "A young girl entering into marriage is still innocent. The realisation of her incapacity to recognise a man as her source of happiness only comes later, after her eyes have been opened. So whoever marries after that realisation is an impostor—oh, disgusting!" And she stood up, agitated.

"One has to try everything once," the doctor laughed cynically.

Minotschka responded with a look of outrage.

"Don't you have any cognac or liqueur?" asked the Jewess, at just the right moment, to lighten the mood. But the hostess could not leave the topic quite yet. She had the table be cleared, folded, and placed in the corner. Then she herself brought out a bottle of cognac, a bottle of ginger liqueur, and cigarettes.

"Whoever prefers beer can have some," she said testily. "There it is." And she pointed to the corner behind the stove, where a row of beer bottles stood.

The Bavarian happily fetched herself a bottle of beer and a glass, Countess Kinzey poured her usual ginger, and Berta Cohn did not abstain from the cognac. The others stood around and lit their cigarettes. The countess smoked silently, leaning back into a corner of the sofa. Involuntarily, Minotschka found herself by her side; and sat down, legs crossed, on the armrest. The Frenchwoman had joined the woman from Berlin by the window. In halting, fragmented French, the tall German gleefully recounted the history of Elise Fritz the turncoat while her hereditary foe[1] listened very keenly.

"The day after tomorrow, Else Lehmann will be taking her doctorate," the doctor began. "Who's coming to the auditorium?"

"I will," "All of us," was the resounding response.

"What is the subject of the dissertation?" the Viennese inquired.

"On the effect of potassium in urine," explained Dr. Tatjana.

"Oh, how horrid," said the Polish woman, smiling.

"Bah, everyone has his hobby-horse," the doctor teased her. "My dissertation considered rectal diseases. You don't find that pleasing? No? Then it is just as well that you study music and not medicine, because in science, there is nothing disgusting and unspeakable, since what exists and manifests itself in diseases proves the means to our knowledge!"

"Certainly," parried the countess, "Only I could never study medicine!"

"Nor could many people," Berta Cohn interrupted. "Even our infallible Minotschka couldn't, otherwise she would not have switched from medicine to philosophy, to literature and art history. My, it always seems to me a bit like starting with a fine Bavarian beer from Munich and then drinking raspberry lemonade!"

"I have my particular reasons," Minotschka said, her voice almost hoarse. "You know what they are as well as I do! Medicine is not responsible for the change in my course of study, the fault lies with the current state of science, the suppression of uncomfortable discoveries! The entire manner of our approach toward the female, whether or not female in thought and feeling, that is what has made the study of medicine impossible for me! Should I have to treat poor, miserable women and girls, whom I could help, if I were allowed to speak, but to whom I am not allowed to speak, because science won't recognise all that it so very well knows? Should I act against my convictions and drive creatures the same as you and me into a man's arms, simply because the world upholds time-honoured traditions, and marriage and sexual congress between a man and a woman constitute the basis for the medical profession? Would you want that?

1 Because of their continual border disputes, Germans and the French have often regarded each other as enemies.

Could you? Aren't doctors, because they won't bring the truth into the light of science, our worst enemies? Couldn't they use true, scientific facts to recast the woman question, which really isn't a woman question at all, but rather a question of the third sex? And you, you who feel like me, you who are called to resist capriciousness and convention, do you possess the sad courage to remain silent? I say 'courage,' because I for one no longer have the courage to bear the current state of affairs without saying anything! In that you have bested me!"

She had turned deathly pale, her dark eyes were shining eerily. Quietly placing her arm around the outraged woman, the countess said only, "Milaya Minotschka!" But today her soothing voice failed in its effect. The agitated woman only pressed her friend's hand and continued to address the women, who were listening with astonishment: "And now all of you, you, Dr. Kassberg, Berta, and you, Zeline: would you dare to write a doctoral dissertation on the scientifically substantiated, positive proof of the existence of a third sex? Would you?"

She took one step toward the woman from Prague.

"'Course not," replied the latter. "No faculty would accept it!"

"I'll try it once, though," joked the woman from Vienna, secretly nudging her Czech compatriot.

"My God," began Dr. Kassberg, "In many ways you are right, dear Fernandoff! But how in the world would you scientifically defend your thesis? Certainly, it's clear that all of us here are perverse women, and there are hundreds and thousands of us. But are we not quite possibly exceptions, we can't claim our own laws, aren't we perhaps only strong intelligent women, whose intellect has lulled or perhaps even deadened our sex, and who consequently cannot at all recognise men as such? Who will scientifically determine that and how will they do so?"

"That is a matter for psychiaters,"[1] Minotschka said. "Even though I, too, find it degrading that we are subject to psychiatric classification. Not even the most unnerving, vulgar roué is accorded that dubious honour."

---

1 A term in use at the turn of the nineteenth century. "Psychiater" appears in Bram's Stoker's *Dracula* (1897), for example. The *OED* includes a reference to "psychiater" Richard Freiherr von Krafft-Ebing (1840–1902), the sexologist whose writings, including his most famous, *Psychopathia Sexualis*, inform *Are They Women?*

"We are still better off than men like us," interjected the doctor. "Look at our fellow sufferers of the male sex, then you'll be content with your lot!"

Now the little actress jumped in: "Oh," she cried out in French. "Oh, Fräulein Fernandoff is so right! Oh, if only I weren't a poor actress, if I had learned, had studied, oh, what wouldn't I do! But as it is! One has to endure every sort of meanness and demand from men; nobody will believe that one can live without a lover, that a man means nothing to us, and never could be more to us than just a person,——oh, it's outrageous! How I hate, hate, hate those men who consider themselves superior to us and think that they are different from us, men who think we exist for them without individuality, without our own character, creatures intended only for their debauchery! Oh, I hate, hate, hate them!"

She rushed to Minotschka and leaned her curly head against the latter's shoulder, as if only she could offer protection and solace. The discussion now became more diffuse. They all talked at once, the tone ever more serious and urgent. A dull sort of grief hung over the small circle, their particular interests seeming to subside in the wake of their recognition of the bond that they shared, their common fate. The little actress's eyes shone brightly, she even cried as she discussed her profession, which prescribed that men's sympathy or at least their benevolence serve as the guiding principle.

For Frau Annie, the conversation was embarrassing. After all, she was the only one who, as far as the outside world was concerned, had a husband. Her entire position was dubious, and in reality—in front of others—it did not allow her to speak as fulsomely as she would have liked. She prepared to leave. The conversation came to a halt. The Frenchwoman, who had only understood the French part of the discussion, was in all likelihood bored, and so she followed Frau Annie's example. The two Germans joined them as well.

Minotschka accompanied her guests to the stairway. Now she returned to the room: "Alright my dears, now we are really amongst ourselves, let's have another drink!" Then retrieving more bottles of wine, she poured them into the large carafes.

"Look, Minotschka," Zeline opined, as she emptied her glass with one draught, "look, you are entirely correct! I'd very much like to write my dissertation on this topic. That will be in two years' time, and who knows how things might have changed by then. At present, it's not possible to demand the impossible.

Even though a few professors would gladly permit it, we're just not for everyone! Cheers!"

She spoke all of this in her soft dialect, her comical mix of High German and Viennese. With it, she always managed to create a conciliatory atmosphere, in contrast to the doctor's sharp tongue, which yielded quite the opposite.

"Certainly," intoned Countess Kinzey now, with elegant calm, "certainly, we must attempt to assert ourselves in public, we must be recognised and not overlooked! The vast majority of people, including the educated classes, have no idea of our existence, our desires, our rights as human beings. Yet, we here are the ones who bear responsibility! We do not stand up for ourselves enough, we do not champion our cause, we do not make it possible for ourselves to be recognised as such, as neither man nor woman. We must be prepared, at any given moment, to advocate for and to prove ourselves, again and again; we cannot afford to allow ourselves to be dismissed as sick or as poseurs or condescendingly treated as especially gifted women. Instead, we must demonstrate that we are the representatives of a mixture, a human species that, without exception manifesting itself as an intellectual elite, is entitled to consideration. But we can only safeguard ourselves insofar as we locate ourselves fearlessly beyond the spheres of actual men and women. We cannot hypocritically misidentify ourselves as we traverse the marketplace of life. It's bad enough that we are compelled to engage in this comedy of errors, whereby we present ourselves as women, subjected to everything women must expect, arranged and ordered as if we were part and parcel of a man's bill of goods!"

"How true your words, dear Marta, how true!" said the hostess. "Oh, one almost despairs when one sees and feels how terribly difficult the struggle is, to present oneself as a woman. Certainly I agree, each one of us who, with conviction, belongs to the third sex has a duty, a sacred duty, to warn those undecided, wavering companions of ours against marriage, to warn those whom we, with a practiced eye and a shared sense of belonging, readily discern. They know nothing of love and life; we must prevent them from making either themselves or any man unhappy. Had, for example, some sympathetic soul recognised and warned me in time, I would not have robbed my former spouse of three years of his life, and I would not have wasted that precious time! Who can measure the agony that women such as we encounter in marriage! If she is not sensual, even the normal woman suffers under the physical aspects of the

conjugal bond! Such a marriage murders the soul! It is imperative to have recognised oneself before marriage, which for a man
is always an adventure and for a woman a danger! That is what
makes marriage, even for normal human beings, a terrible risk.
Both parties enter into an emotional and physical relationship
without any sort of proven competence, and so, in countless
cases, meet with shipwreck. Should the foundation of the state
rest on these rotten, unhealthy connections, should a love of
work and morality spring from them? Nowadays in marriage,
conditions breed a proletariat of love that, in its brutal excesses
against the personal freedom of the one or the other spouse,
poorly hides itself behind civilisation's magic cloak of morality.
As this brutality increases, the more unpleasant are the consequences of the marriage, the more depressing and oppressive
they become. The heaviest anguish lies with the aesthetic consequences. Insofar as the one or the other party regards himself as
continually wounded in his love of beauty, in his tenderness or
in his aesthetic sensibility, if, because of the way it is carried out,
the smallest, most insignificant action becomes odious, and
causes him emotional pain, manifesting itself even in physical
discomfort, marriage becomes a terrible martyrdom, which,
without the possibility of liberation, can lead to rage and
murder! Even under propitious social circumstances, wounded
aesthetic sensibility allows for neither a sexual nor a moral
union." Minotschka fell silent and lowered her gaze. Once she
began to speak, her words carried her away. She spoke convincingly and with enthusiasm, it was a pleasure to listen to her.
Moreover, the seriousness of the day's topic under discussion
captivated every single one of these intelligent women.
    "You are quite right, dear Fernandoff," the medical resident
remarked suddenly. "We medical doctors all know as much,
though we cannot publicly disclose it. If we did, no one would
want to marry anymore! The majority of all women's nervous
disorders and neuroses can be solely attributed to the perfidious
sexual relations that marriage imposes. Women are left in ignorance about the most natural things and then ridiculed, mocked,
and damned as 'shrews,' an endless legion of hysterics! Furthermore, they are held responsible for their condition and these
psychically and physically tortured beings are told to exercise
restraint. A man in a similar situation is pitied as a neurasthenic,
he is at least categorised in terms of a respectable classification
of illnesses. By contrast, poor, suffering married women manifest
a wide array of character abnormalities, which any doctor, if only

he wanted to, could clearly recognise as betraying his female patients' condition. But we are not allowed to recognise as much, even though it is in our own self-interest! Many a woman freed from the brutalities of the marital bedroom, and simply allowed to work as a human being, and so to stand on her own two feet, would prove a capable and useful individual, almost each and every one of them would!"

"I'm just thinking," interrupted the Viennese, "that a sensible person would never get engaged in such foolish love twaddle. A mind shaped by mature understanding and serious profound knowledge would never permit such a befuddling love! When I hear about the crime, folly, and silliness committed in the name of love, I always question whether lovers have any common sense. Leave me out of this love business!"[1]

Minotschka thoughtfully offered her opinion. "The term 'love' does not seem to me to be quite right. After all, what we so poetically call 'love' is always only a more or less strongly developed sexual drive. I believe that love is actually only a physical pleasure or displeasure; a person with pronounced intelligence would always have to experience true love, as one says. I am speaking now only of normally feeling women and men, but I believe that a person who is energetically and intensively intellectually engaged does not have time to think that much about the fulfillment of love. I would even assert that a working, well-balanced person does not have time for unhappy love; that is a sickness for the mentally deranged and for wastrels!"

"I am of the same opinion," the doctor laughingly agreed. "Most average women suffer from both a lack of occupation and an uneducated mind, and as a consequence readily become the victims of unhappy love. This manner of aberration is diseased, and it is high time to adopt a worthwhile purpose and to respond to non-physiological representations in novels and the shallow and senseless glorification of unhappy lovers, who should be treated as the simple, sick people they actually are. Prolonged, unhappy love can seriously harm life and health and must be energetically combatted. One must enlighten the ill, call upon their sense of honour, and show them their own pathetic longing in such a way, that they recognise their own unworthiness and are ashamed."

"Bravo, bravo," shouted the merry little woman from Prague. "Bravo, bravo! I completely agree! Considered logically, love

---

1 In the original, this speech is written in Viennese dialect.

only has worth and a right to existence, insofar as it is mutual. Only then is it a natural feeling. Yes, yes, at the outset love is beautiful, pleasant, pleasant when it endures, and ugly when it ends!"

"I don't know if all of you are right," said the actress, somewhat embarrassed. "I am not an educated, learned woman as all of you are; unlike Fräulein Fernandoff I cannot make any pretty speeches. Given what you have just said, I would have to have a taste for love! And yet that is not the case! For me, love remains something foreign, and man is only a meaningless term! I believe this is something that lies solely in ourselves: women like us can never love a man as a man, all of nature's various gradations of womanhood will love differently! For this reason, I find that there is nothing more false than to term all the various feelings of affection or devotion love! I simply believe that love deprives one of freedom, and it is of the utmost importance to uphold the freedom of the self!"

Dr. Kassberg heartily clapped her hands. "Look at our Pierrette!" she scoffed. "The chrysalis is becoming a butterfly!"

Then she condescendingly stroked the actress's hand.

"One o'clock," remarked the Polish woman suddenly, as the bell in the nearby church struck with a dull sound.

Everyone prepared to leave. Little more was said. Plans for the next day were discussed, and then the ladies parted. Countess Kinzey stayed back a bit. Standing in the doorway, she pressed Minotschka to her and kissed her hair. "Good night, my darling," she said. "I'll expect you tomorrow night!" Then she hurried after the others.

For a while Minotschka hesitated on the landing. "Oh well then," she murmured with a smile. "Then I will just go to sleep. They are all too respectable!"

During the vacation period Minotschka, along with Countess Kinzey and Berta Cohn, had taken a trip to the Bernese Highlands;[1] and as she loved Interlaken[2] more than anything, it was there the friends decided to spend the last weeks of their holidays. There, however, the woman from Prague met a married cousin with whom she travelled northward. Minotschka and Marta could now continue to live wholly according to their taste. They photographed, they chatted in naive fashion of harmless

---

1 In the canton of Bern, the Bernese Highlands include some of the most stunning mountains in Switzerland, such as the Jungfrau and the Eiger.

2 A popular Swiss resort town.

matters, and, for a while, played the role of women with nothing to do and wishing to do nothing. All in all delightful, the weeks and days happily came to a close as the women who were used to work began to find them a bit confining.

Upon their return to Geneva all sorts of surprises awaited them. A young relation of the countess had taken up lodging in a boarding school and was awaiting her cousin's visit. Moreover, Marta's elderly father, who was staying in Aix-les-Bains[1] and taking a cure, urgently requested his daughter's presence.

Minotschka also was met with two unpleasant pieces of news. One letter contained the request of a very sick Russian woman staying in Clarens: Minotschka, with whom she still had many things to settle, should come as soon as possible to her, as she was nearing her end. The other letter came from a young doctor, who had proposed to Minotschka soon after her divorce. She had rejected his marriage offer, but he apparently, not knowing the woman's reasons, wanted, after a lengthy respectable waiting period, to propose anew. Minotschka found this latter situation very embarrassing, and she regarded it as a happy coincidence that her visit to the sick Russian woman would excuse her and relieve her of receiving the annoying visitor. Dr. Laum wrote, he was only passing through, would not be able to stop for long, and that he would on such and such a day call on her. She took the Russian woman's letter, added a few explanatory words, and instructed her landlady to hand it over to her visitor. Then she went to find Marta, told her about the trip to Clarens, and after bringing the countess to the train, cycled along the lake toward Clarens.

It was a splendid, warm October day, and Minotschka blissfully experienced the benefit of robust exercise. Because of Marta, who was very pampered and averse to any sort of effort, she had in the last while neglected cycling. Today the unaccustomed and long denied pleasure doubled her enjoyment, and she readily surrendered herself to the blissfully peaceful feeling of gliding soundlessly and speedily through the glorious countryside. Particularly after strenuous intellectual work, the weakness in her ankle prevented her from any lengthy walking, while bicycle riding occasioned no such problem. Now and then, she encountered a group of cycling Englishwomen that, without so much as a word, raced past her like a wild hunting party.

---

1 A famous French spa town.

Towards evening she arrived in Clarens, where she found her former classmate in the last stage of consumption. Following the sick woman's wishes, she tirelessly wrote letters to relatives and acquaintances, the lawyer, and the Russian consulate. With admirable strength, the suffering woman directed the course of her last days, carefully putting in order everything that with her death could result in mistakes. The women continued to sit together for a long time, and when after two days she left, Minotschka knew that she would never again see her sick friend. A light, warm rain fell, as a leaden heaviness lay over Lake Geneva; struck to the core, shocked by her experience, Minotschka made use of the steamboat for the return trip; in her state of mind, cycling would have been impossible. She also did not go directly home, particularly since she assumed that Dr. Laum might still pay her a visit; instead, she went in search of Berta Cohn; the merry woman from Prague was just the person to help her overcome her present melancholy. Only on the next day did she return home; work was calling. She had lost four days, and nothing takes its toll like the disruption of one's habitual work and circumstances; she lacked spirit and zeal. She read the correspondence that she had received, and in the process discovered a card from Dr. Laum, who had in mind to pay her a visit that very day. So she could not avoid him! She was really miserable: Marta Kinzey's absence was putting her even more out of sorts than she had anticipated, as with a vague fear she thought that her friend was staying away longer than intended. And on top of everything this Dr. Laum! If only she had taken Berta with her in order to prevent any intimate conversation! There was a knock! It was Frau Annie, who wanted to call on Minotschka. Following on her heels was Boris Karaschneff, a medical doctor, and the only male friend, whom Minotschka was always happy to see. Already in Leipzig they had seen a great deal of each other and had become good friends. The student felt a burden falling from her: "You've come at just the right time," she said brightly. "A gentleman is supposed to pay me a visit later, and I ask you both, please do not leave me until he has gone!"

"With pleasure," said the Russian. Without allowing her to discern as much, he harboured great affection and admiration for Minotschka; essentially he was jealous of every man acquainted with his friend.

"Should one be kind or rude towards him," he asked, ready for a fight.

"But, Boris," Minotschka rang out, "how can you ask such a thing! Very kind, of course, since the gentleman would be a very pleasant sort of person, if, if he—"

"If he weren't in love with you!" Boris concluded. Everyone laughed. In that moment, the servant brought in Dr. Laum's card; Minotschka only received her small circle of intimates informally.

She went to meet her visitor and greeted him with a friendly though reserved manner. Introductions were made. Dr. Laum looked at the visitors with apparent annoyance. "I have already been to visit you twice, Madam," he said, "but I hear that you were travelling; and now I seem to be intruding once again!"

"Absolutely not," protested Minotschka. "On the contrary, I am pleased to introduce my dear friends to you!"

There was a bit of mischievousness in the look she gave Boris, but Dr. Laum did not pay any attention to it.

She had sherry and glasses brought. Then she held up her filled glass toward the doctor and in obviating fashion said, "So, dear Herr Laum, now that we have met once again, drink to my future. That brings luck! That I will remain as happy in my life of freedom, as I am now!" The glasses clinked together, the doctor looked abashed.

"To your happiness, yes," he said. "But not as you know it now, but rather at the side of a beloved husband!"

For someone in his situation, that remark was the most disadvantageous he could have made. Nothing more outraged Minotschka, this strong independent being, than the observation that a husband was the source of all happiness. She always perceived it as an insult, as an underestimation of her worth, and as a result, given her temperament, she became inconsiderate, even rude. She rose to her feet.

"Dear doctor," she said forcefully. "Permit me to tell you something: stop with these phrases! Once and for all, I don't want to hear them! You are an old acquaintance and as much as your visit gives me pleasure, you would spoil this hour for me, were you not to speak sensibly!"

"But, Madam!" he stammered, deeply dismayed. "Do not call me that," she cried out, now really indignant. "According to our laws I had to discard the name of my erstwhile spouse after the divorce. When I did so, I also cast off the rest. I am only Minotschka Fernandoff, the student!"

"Well, then how am I to address you?" he asked, profoundly shocked.

"Frau or Fräulein Fernandoff," she scoffed. "Whichever you please!" The doctor was apparently undecided whether he should go or stay. But he saw that Frau Annie, who had had no idea of the visitor's intentions, was also looking at her companion disapprovingly. That made him decide to stay. He put aside his ill humour and, changing his course, asked, "How is Fräulein Zeline Ardy? Where in Geneva does she live?"

"Zeline has gone to Zurich for the semester," Minotschka explained, happy to be able to turn the conversation. "And what about your sister? Is she still at the Leipzig Conservatory?"

"Oh, no," responded the doctor. "She was not supposed to study music! She only took lessons in order to pass the time, like all young girls, until they can fulfill their true vocation."

"So is your Fräulein sister engaged?" asked Frau Annie in part out of politeness and because she saw that Minotschka was ready with a sharp retort.

"Oh, no," he responded naively. "But she hasn't given up the hope of marrying; she is still only twenty-four years old. And now a number of gentlemen are interested in her; I think one or the other will avail himself. As we no longer have parents, Marianne is at the moment visiting an aunt!"

"Good gracious!" Minotschka called out, jumping to her feet. "Is that ever disgraceful! Don't girls today have any shred of honour?"

The doctor pulled back, startled.

"What do you mean?" he asked, uncertain.

"What do I mean?" taunted Minotschka. "Now that's not difficult to understand! I find it dishonourable and humiliating to raise a girl for marriage from her earliest years, without recognising her individuality, to train her in the hunt for a man, instead of offering her an honest means of earning her daily bread. Don't you feel the shame you are imposing on your sister, when you describe how she still hopes that 'something' will succeed? So she would accept just anyone, whoever presents himself?"

It was becoming ever more unpleasant for the doctor, who was no longer certain how he should respond.

"But surely all women should and want to marry!" he again protested.

"Should and want?" Frau Annie now began to speak. "No, Herr Doctor, that is just not quite right! All of us do not want to marry, neither should we nor shall we in the future. Since first and foremost we are all human beings and then only reproductive beings.[1] All reproductive beings are of course human beings, but not all human beings are reproductive beings."

"I don't quite understand you!" said the doctor. "And even if women don't really want to and shouldn't marry, there's nothing else for them to do! A girl can't remain a burden to her parents or her relatives forever. Isn't it terrible to be an old maid?"

"Certainly," Minotschka replied. "It must be terrible to be an old maid whose humanity has died away and whose life is made up of only a demoralising toadyism. For a woman who has been passed over, there are first of all her parents, who must support her much longer than they would want, then either the brother or the brother-in-law, who plays the role of provider, then relatives, and if they don't have anything or if there aren't any, then the community or the state has to step in to take care of the sick, old spinsters. Fortunately, one doesn't yet let them meet their end on the streets, that's still worth a good deal!" she scoffed.

"Russians agree with you completely," offered Boris, now inserting himself into the discussion. "In Russia such an old Fräulein is called 'prizheevalka,'[2] that is, someone who moves from place to place for food and shelter."

---

1   In her 1897 essay "Intellektuelle Grenzlinien zwischen Mann und Frau" ("Intellectual Boundaries between Man and Woman"), in which she argues that women should be granted access to higher education, Helene Lange (1848–1930) distinguishes between men as reproductive beings and women as nurturing, maternal beings. In the novel, Frau Annie seems familiar with this kind of argument, even as she departs from it. She distinguishes between those women who reproduce and those who do not in order to underscore the importance of women's education and so their access to a range of professions. The term used in the same way appears again in Adelt-Duc's *Indische Novellen* (1914).

2   An old-fashioned term. It comes from the root word жить (*zhit'*, or *zheet'*), to live. The combination of this root word with the prefix *pri* modifies the word to mean somebody who came (from the outside) and settled in (прижиться [*prizhit'sja*]—"to settle in, to fit in"). A *prizhee-valka* was a poor woman (but not a serf or peasant) who lived in and was supported by a wealthy household. She was not tasked with any specific chores; her main responsibilities were to keep the lady of the house company and to entertain her. A *prizheevalka* could be a woman who used to be wealthy, but lost money, became poor, and was taken into the wealthy household out of charity. The more general meaning of the word describes somebody who lives at other people's expense, who serves, and tends to somebody for bread. It usually bears some negative context. The male equivalent is *prizheeval*.

The Russian's good-natured teasing annoyed the doctor. He now went on the attack. "My God," he remarked with apparent calm, "it may well be as you say; still, I believe that only emancipated women oppose marriage and support an occupational pursuit. And we can't follow their lead, since emancipation, in its true essence, is, after all, the negation of marriage! Unfeminine women are an abomination for everyone!"

"Without question!" said Minotschka.

"So what, then?" asked Laum with surprise.

"'Unfeminine women' holds different meanings for us," she offered. "For what is this term 'femininity'? A wish that, dictated and sustained by a man, molds a woman according to his taste. Hence, it is based on a confusion of cause and effect, whereby women whom men find quite feminine, are described as such. Yet, these women are in actuality the contrary, the 'unfeminine ones,' given that they live only according to a man's wishes and pretensions. The true 'feminine' ones would therefore be those women who maintain their own individuality and constitute their own particular species psychically and physically. Certainly, a woman who is a mother is 'feminine,' without question. Yet no woman thinks initially of motherhood when she is trying to win a husband."

"Yes, but how does one then discover that so-called 'femininity'?" Laum asked, with more and more interest. "How do you imagine it?"

Minotschka, having folded her hands in her lap, looked down at them thoughtfully. "I have my own method," she smiled. "I assume that every healthy female should be raised to learn an occupation, just as a man is. Everyone according to her abilities! Some would become craftswomen, others would devote themselves to business, others again to office work, to study, to teaching, to art! Later the parties would separate without any discord and hate, some in order to find their happiness in marriage, the others, who were not of that mind, to stand as free human beings on their own two feet. No risk would lie therein, since disposition would decide, and the number of those wanting to marry would always be larger than that of the others. In this way, however, countless women for whom marriage is a torment would be freed, while marriage in turn would also benefit, as it would only receive its well-disposed entities."

"But I believe that many women marry because they do not want to work, do not, shall we say, have the courage to stand up for themselves!" offered Laum.

"Certainly," responded Frau Annie with zeal, "more than one thinks. But that lies solely with a faulty upbringing. In order for a woman today to make her way in life and assure herself of an occupation, she needs courage!"

"My view is the same as my friend's," Boris added. "I, too, say that every woman should be raised to have an occupation that befits her abilities and talents, her social circumstances and those of her health. Only in this way can she be later spared difficult psychic conflicts. To be sure, her upbringing would be her first introduction to vocational life and only upon its completion would the free choice of pursuits become her right! For, after all, marriage is neither for man nor for woman a specific occupation, but rather only a safety valve that the state has established for itself!"

"Oh, but good heavens," Laum protested, "then women would become our competitors in all fields!"

Minotschka laughed out loud and clapped her hands. "Of course!" she teased. "And would they! Cato himself already said, 'As soon as women become our equals, they will become stronger than us and will subjugate us!'[1] Do you see?"

"Well, I do not doubt women's capability," offered the doctor. "But with that I want to say that the competition with woman will make man's struggle for existence more difficult, and he will be increasingly less able to marry easily!"

"An eternally vicious circle," said Minotschka. "Certainly women's competition is to be feared, but my principle is just this: the right of the fittest! Not the person who is physically most fit but rather the one who is intellectually most so! Whether man or woman—only intelligence, and not one's sex, has rights! Ability must decide! Certainly from day to day and from year to year the struggle for survival becomes more difficult, and in fact mainly because of the refinement of intellectual abilities. The individual must struggle mightily to achieve little! And in order to maintain what he has achieved, he must always be constantly ready to do battle, so that no one else overtakes him. Let us fight this battle, dear doctor—intelligence is the trump card!"

---

1 The quotation from Cato the Elder (234–149 BCE) is often translated as follows: "Suffer women once to arrive at an equality with you, and they will from that moment become your superiors" (as recorded in Livy, *History of Rome* 24.3). See Livy, *History of Rome*, Books. XXXI–XXXIV, translated by Evan T. Sage (Harvard UP, 1935), Loeb Classic Library 295. 431.

"You speak excellently," laughed the doctor with a sour-sweet expression on his face, "but with your theories you also leave no sunny side to life! If all of us only want to fight, then we do away with all of life's outward beauty. Then we are left with only one realisation: life is work, work and acquisition! But work and acquisition alone, whether they move in higher intellectual spheres or are perpetuated by manual labour cannot possibly take the place of poetry and happiness for us!"

"By no means," responded Minotschka with agitation. "You are throwing out the baby with the bath water! On the contrary, I hope for much more from life's outward beauty when I assume that all people delight in creating, that the paths that lead to research and knowledge are open to everyone and that those paths give them the possibility to make use of their energy and intelligence and that they are thereby able, according to their individuality and inclination, to obtain for themselves the beautiful things in life that especially entice them."

"I also think that you have forgotten what we previously said," offered Annie, seizing the opportunity to speak. "You want to place women at the centre of life as if they were the most beautiful thing, and you think we want to rob you of that! But we expressly emphasised earlier, the majority of women will always pursue marriage, only perhaps one consistent with more worthy, purposeful provisions. But on the other hand, we want to leave everyone their personal, intellectual, and physical freedom, and to uphold for us women who are not reproductive beings our rights as human beings!"

"Conceded," said Laum. "What you are saying is fully justified. But I only fear that woman with the passage of time will continue to change ever more, so that in the end, when we marry we will be dining daily with our wives in the pub, and that woman as 'the keeper of the hearth' will soon become a myth. Such an undomestic life would end any sociability in the home! The term 'housewife' then would soon be annulled."

"Good heavens, yes, the passage of time and progress would entail as much!" explained Frau Annie. "Our sociability today has become very different, much freer! It demands and offers more than before, yet in so doing lessening women's load. Nowadays public houses entice not only men, but also frequently women: married couples take their meals together in pubs and read their newspapers! Meet their acquaintances! In this way one doesn't have to make any social concessions, one comes and goes as one wishes! And then, for example," she continued, "how pleasant it is to hold a big celebration or party outside the home! Almost all of my acquaintances do as much! One spares oneself thereby so much agitation, inconvenience, and responsibility! And how this relieves a woman especially, since she is the one who agonises over the preparation of every celebration. Consider for a moment, Herr Doctor, it is really very practical: one entertains one's friends at a favourite hotel, and the risks regarding the dishes offered and the inadequacy of the servants fall away, and for all of which—one achieves one's enjoyment at less expense and then returns home to a house that one finds unchanged! No commotion, no upheaval, the house-wife goes to the party like every other guest!"

"But you do need to recognise," Laum cried out, "that women consequently lose the ideal value of domesticity, not to speak of its practical value! Domesticity's hearth will become ever more monotonous, dreary, and forsaken!"

"That it will," replied Minotschka, "because already today it cannot compete with what is offered outside of the home. Slowly but surely public sociability is pulling the modern world into its orbit!"

"Hell's bells," laughed the doctor, half in earnest, half amused. "Then it would be foolish to marry!"

"Certainly! Naturally, we agree with you," was the resounding response.

With that the conversation shifted into a bantering mode. They discussed various things, and the doctor, perhaps with his ardour seriously cooled, perhaps also with the realisation that there was nothing that he could do, made ready to depart.

"My best wishes for your future, most revered lady," he said, taking Minotschka's hand and pressing it. "I do not imagine that we shall see each other again! You fly toward the sun, while I remain earth-bound! May you always be happy!"

His voice tremored slightly and Minotschka, too, was moved. "All the best to you," she said warmly. "And, rest assured, it will always give me pleasure to hear from you!"

A final pressing of her hand, a bow to the others. He was gone.

"Thank heavens," Boris called out with amusement. "The enemy has been vanquished!" But he moved back in alarm when Minotschka turned abruptly: "I will not tolerate any mockery of Dr. Laum," she remarked curtly.

"Hmm, hmm," uttered the Russian, but he said nothing more.

"Tonight I am going to a terrace concert."[1] Annie resumed. "Are you coming, Minotsch?"

"Yes," the other said immediately, for she was in no mood to work.

"May I join you as well?" joked Boris, folding his hands together in entreaty.

"Naturally," laughed Minotschka, disarmed. "Let's go!"—— The evening was glorious, anyone who could was spending it outdoors. There were throngs of listeners on the concert terraces, all tables were overflowing: a jolly, chattering crowd surged between the rows. The three friends looked around for available seating. All of a sudden, somebody called out to them! Sitting at a large corner table were their acquaintances, Dr. Tatjana Kassberg; her cousin Mischah Statsky; a female Russian dentist, whose scholarship everyone doubted, but not the fact that she was Mischah's mistress; Berta Cohn, the actress; and Fräulein Dr. Reuter, a young German woman as serious as she was learned. A large punchbowl sat on the table, everyone appeared to be in high spirits. "Well, well," asked Boris, immediately sensing the unusual mood. "What is going on here?"

Everyone spoke at once, but the Jewess drowned them all out. "As of today, Tatjana is a permanent resident physician at the hospital," she yelled out. "She is taking over from Fräulein Reuter, who is leaving for Bern to be engaged as a primary medical resident there!"

They congratulated Tatjana and joined her at the table. "Waiter, more glasses," Tatjana called. "We need to toast the sciences!"

"But for me, a glass of Löwenbräu beer," Minotschka called. "You have to excuse me, dear Tatjana," she addressed the Russian, "but as you know, I have an aversion to all things sweet! I'll still drink to your health, even if it's with beer, after all, it's not the type of beverage that matters!" The new resident physician did not reply, she sat cowering on her chair. Her small, dark, sharp-eyed Tartar face, peeking out of the bizarre, red apron-style dress she wore, appeared strangely foreign. She kept encouraging everyone to drink, while she herself wearily sipped a cup of tea into which she squeezed a whole lemon!

"How is your beloved countess doing?" she asked Minotschka very suddenly. "Will she be returning soon?"

---

1 Terrace concerts are, as the name suggests, held outside and offer audiences tiered seating.

"I don't know," the other woman answered, uncomfortable with the question. "She has not written me yet! Besides, I was gone, I went to Clarens, calling on Zinaida Wergewsky: she is nearing her end and will hardly survive this week. She knows it, the poor thing, yet she is conducting herself heroically!"

"That's because she was born in Siberia to a heroic mother, who wouldn't let her husband go into exile by himself," the doctor brusquely replied.

"She should not have gone to Munich when she did," Dr. Reuter commented. "She should have stayed in Crimea. Now she is dying on foreign soil, in a dreary sanatorium, without a human soul shedding a tear for her."

"What good will tears do her," Tatjana scoffed with a cynical smile. "What's dead is dead! I, too, had a young woman die under my hands today, she had been lying in agony for months. And over there, at the third table, there is her husband! Do you see him shedding any tears?"

They all looked over at the table, where the unusual husband was apparently sitting, and frowned.

"My God," shrugged Minotschka, "the poor devil may well have gotten accustomed to the illness. One can get accustomed to anything, even to the illness of one's beloved, which estranges us anyway. Since the person we loved was healthy, was another person."

The little actress, who was rather tender-hearted, hated this type of conversation among the physicians. She approached Minotschka resolutely.

"Fräulein Fernandoff," she asked, "would you mind accompanying me through the gardens for a short stroll? I wish to share some things with you."

"If you wish," replied Minotschka, rising from her chair with little enthusiasm. Pierette linked arms with the student and steered her towards the more secluded parts of the garden.

"I really do have to share something important with you," she began timidly. "But please, do not get cross with me!"

"Nonsense," answered the student brusquely. "Speak, and don't give such elaborate introductions!"

She was always this brusque, almost brutal, towards timid women. She hated anything apathetic.

"Do tell me first," the actress hesitantly pleaded, "will you be going to Germany for the next summer semester?"

Anxiously, she looked up at her much taller companion.

"Yes," Minotschka answered curtly, "to Munich or Berlin. But what does that have to do with your situation?"

"Dear Minotschka," the girl began ingratiatingly, "I only wanted to ask you to take me with you! Please understand me: I wish to leave the stage! I have been thinking about it for a long time, and so I thought, perhaps I could teach French and give piano lessons in Germany——or maybe find a position——but not all on my own——I would go, with you——if you'd like," she added quietly.

Minotschka did not say anything, she just whistled through her teeth, as she always did when her mind was occupied with something extraordinary.

For a while, Pierette kept hoping for her friend's response. But when she simply kept on whistling, the actress said, half in tears: "But come what may, either way, I will not continue with the stage! Better to be a servant than that! I cannot stand watching all that posturing any longer, listening to those speeches, following the advice that is all purely geared toward men! I cannot find any interest in any man, I cannot become like all the others, it all disgusts me so horribly, ah, so horribly! You have no idea how we are faring, Minotschka, you, in your position of privilege and freedom! Oh, if only I were a boy, a man, how I would show those men, and how I would hate those women, those weak, unprincipled beings who only know men, and when it comes to men, know their wallets best!" She paused with exhaustion and forcefully gripped Minotschka's arm. But the other woman was still not speaking; she stared at the ground in front of her.

"So you don't want to?" the actress finally called out, indignantly. "Just tell me!"

"Silly little goose," the other woman then laughed, her deep alto voice even darker than usual. "You foolish little thing!" And she tenderly embraced Pierette.

"Won't you allow me time to think? Yes? Anyway, I already know the most important thing! I shall not say anything but this: be ready to leave in March, I shall take you with me!"

"Minotschka, oh, Minotschka," cried the other, "truly, you truly want to?" With sudden humility, she took the student's hand and kissed it tenderly.

"I shall be indebted to you forever," she pledged, and her narrow little doll face turned pale. "I am yours from now on, do with me what you will!"

"There, there," Minotschka fended her off with a smile. "No human being must voluntarily deprive himself of freedom! I only wish to protect you until you can stand on your own two feet, I only want to rescue and sustain the human being within you. That is after all no less than our duty! But let's return to the matter at hand," she remarked. "You should give your director notice now, and then, in the meantime, my dearest, do learn some German! You should not be entirely dependent on me later on. As soon as I know whether I will go to Munich or to Berlin, I will begin to arrange things in your best interest, you can rely on me entirely in this regard! I would love nothing more than to go to Heidelberg! But that ideal university town offers too many easy distractions from work, and we both must be truly dedicated to our work! It is settled, then," and she offered her hand to the little one, who clasped it wordlessly.

In the meantime they had returned to their table and their companions. Dismayed, Minotschka noticed that their two empty seats had been taken by strangers. They were men in the prime of life, apparently members of Geneva's middle class.

"Why did you let them take our seats?" inquired Minotschka quietly.

"We could not help it," Boris replied. "They said they would leave as soon as the ladies returned."

Indeed, the strangers stood up in order to leave. Merely out of politeness, they all protested, and so when Fräulein Dr. Reuter, Mischah, and the dentist were rising to leave, the gentlemen gratefully remained seated. The punchbowl had been emptied and Tatjana ordered tea for everyone. "But with cognac," Berta Cohn urged.

"With cognac," echoed the doctor.

During the intermissions, the conversation turned lively; as soon as the music intoned,[1] however, everyone fell silent. This was because Minotschka, like the other Russians, was very musical. She adored any sort of music as a kind of elixir of life. Moreover, the orchestra displayed a noticeable preference for Slavic melodies.

When the music ended, they decided to stay a little while longer. Beautiful days, such as this October day, were surely numbered; beneath the terrace, Lake Geneva lay dark, as if it

---

1   The original German includes a typographical error here. The text reads *internierte* (interned). The word should be *intonierte* (intoned).

had slid back into the distance; the stars twinkled, bright and shining. Across the water sped small boats decked out with lanterns, and brightly lit steamboats puffing mightily. From faraway they could hear songs. A lone light, strangely enticing, flickered across from Jean-Jacques Rousseau Island.

The mood of the small group became even lighter, when suddenly, after an incidental remark, the two strangers interrupted the conversation. "You must be studying medicine?" one of them suddenly addressed Dr. Kassberg. He had gathered this from the conversation.

"I am a physician, yes," she replied with reticence.

"Oh, how extraordinarily interesting," one of them said. "We are Germans, and in our country, university-educated women are still a rarity."

The gentlemen casually introduced themselves. The talk more or less covered any number of topics, including the role of women in private and public life. And quite unexpectedly the younger gentleman asked Tatjana adroitly: "Do say, esteemed Fräulein, doesn't the presence of women in the hospitals lead to all sorts of romantic incidents?"

He said this with a suggestive wink of the eye.

"Not at all," came the curt reply. "The gravity of the situation does not allow for anything unimportant."

The questioner felt himself rebuked, but that spurred him on to further debate.

"But I mean," he said, seeking to obviate, "that a woman who has spent years at the university, in the hospital, and in anatomy studies, cannot possibly maintain her feminine charm. She must surely become serious and austere, opinionated and pedantic, arrogant in her sense of self-importance, and, as a rival to men, incapable of love as well as friendship. She cannot help but see men as her competition, and as they are far better equipped than she for battle, see them as just an enemy!"

"Is that all?" Tatjana asked.

"No," he responded, impassioned anew. "I believe that the educated woman is unfit for marriage, for she will value her study over her household!"

"Certainly," Minotschka agreed, "that's why we are not going to marry! I am completely of your opinion that a tender, devoted, feminine woman can never become a doctor or accomplish anything else of significance in public life. Those women belong inside the house, and they will also feel most comfortable at home. Please do not mistake us for those esteemed women—we constitute a different category altogether!"

"Yes, but, good heavens," said the older gentleman, now pensive. "You are women, after all! And if a woman truly wants to, she will always find a field suited to her capabilities! For example diaconal work[1]——"

Minotschka's chair quickly turned around. "You are forgetting one more thing," she said coldly. "Two professions are always open to a woman: both diaconal work and—prostitution! The one merely offers a path of suffering reserved for the faithful, marked by selflessness, patience, and the oppression of one's individuality. The other, through the surrendering of their physical being, assures women of an age-old trade, one that has been left to them, without any objection!"

The men shifted around uncomfortably.

"So any woman with a capacity for subjugation, suffering, and faith should become a deaconess, and a woman who does not want as much,——a harlot?" Minotschka continued mercilessly. "These are the alpha and the omega of life. And marriage is placed somewhere in between the two!"

"That is not what we mean," resumed the stranger exasperatingly. "But marriage should occur, every woman should have to find a husband!"

"Please," Boris mocked, "then introduce polygyny."[2]

"We don't want that!" the speaker retorted.

"But it is not that despicable at all," Dr. Kassberg responded. "I lived among the Ottomans for a long time, and I have to admit that women's lack of freedom is no worse among the Mohammedans with their polygyny than in the Occident with its ostensible freedom. Only the packaging differs!"

"Yes, that's how it is," Boris agreed. "Here, like there, women sell themselves in order to guarantee their food and shelter! But

---

1 A reference to the Lutheran charitable work that, historically, principally engaged women. The man is voicing a familiar argument made by opponents to German women's access to higher education.

2 While writers in the late nineteenth and early twentieth centuries typically used the term polygamy to refer to the practice of having more than one wife, the term actually applies to husbands as well. We have chosen to use the word polygyny as it refers specifically to women and was in use by the mid-nineteenth century. The term in German is gender specific, *Vielweiberei*.

at least the Oriental woman, in offering the same services, is safe from repudiation and abandonment!"[1]

"We are digressing," commented one of the gentlemen. "As far as the question of university studies is concerned, Lombroso, too, is of the opinion that mental labour, the strenuous higher level of occupation, ruins the female's nerves.[2] Consider how many hysterical women there are!"

"But, my good sir," the doctor then snarled while calmly stirring her tea, "You are judging this as a mere lay person! You are simply parroting what you have heard! As a doctor, I must inform you that the majority of hysterical, neurotic, so-called misunderstood women are in fact married women. Almost without exception, they have fallen victim to psychic imbalances only because the lack of productive, satisfying occupation, intellectual enlightenment, and emotional education is taking its toll. The strengthening of one's character and training of one's mind are the surest means of preventing hysteria. For the amorous obsessions of hysterical women almost never originate from a strong sensual need, but stem from an unhealthily agitated fantasy. Our famous Dr. Krafft-Ebing already said as much, that these women love merely out of a feeling of complaisance, to fill up their mental solitude, it has less to do with the physical body!"[3]

---

1 Kassberg's and Boris's comparisons here reflect a standard move made by nineteenth- and early-twentieth-century women's rights supporters across Europe and anglophone North America. The comparison is meant to shock its audience by arguing that women living in "modern" Western countries are no more free than their counterparts living in ostensibly "less civilized" Islamic societies that practice polygyny.

2 Cesare Lombroso (1835–1909), Italian criminologist and physician. His *La donna delinquente, la prostituta e la donna normale* (1893), co-authored with Guglielmo Ferrero, was published in German in 1894. The 1895 English version offered only a partial translation; *The Female Offender* focused on the first part of the text. Only in 2004 did a full English translation become available.

3 In *Über gesunde und kranke Nerven* (*Concerning Healthy and Diseased Nerves*, 1885), pioneer of the study of human sexuality Richard Freiherr von Krafft-Ebing writes, "The view prevalent in lay circles that [a woman's] nonfulfillment of the role that nature has prescribed for her induces illness is a wholly unjustified prejudice. When older virgins are frequently hysterical, the cause is moral rather than physical. Unmarried women who, as an equivalent of marriage, have a serious occupation engaging spirit and mind ... are rarely hysterical" (our translation). We have removed an errant quotation mark from Duc's sentence.

The older one of the strangers laughed and responded mockingly. "Thank God that we do not understand your views!" he said with annoyance. "But apropos Krafft-Ebing! Isn't he the one who speaks up for perverted human beings?"

He proudly glanced around the table.

"Certainly," Minotschka replied, "that's the one, the author of the book *Psychopathia Sexualis*,[1] which most lay people and the uninitiated devour with greed and lasciviousness!"

The friends laughed furtively, the strangers did not reply. Then they whispered among themselves, paid the waiter just then passing by, and stood up.

"Good evening!" they said politely but coolly to the circle, as if they had never exchanged a word with them. Everyone burst out laughing.

"We showed them!" cheered Berta Cohn.

"A pity," Minotschka commented. "I would have loved to enlighten them further! I wanted to tell them that we, too, belong to those 'Krafft-Ebing types'! I think they would have fainted!"

They stayed a little longer, and after the others had said goodbye, the doctor joined Minotschka. They did not live so far from each other. Today, Dr. Kassberg seemed rather keen on accompanying her friend. While they were engaged in a lively discussion on a deserted street, the student heard someone's footsteps behind them. She turned around and encountered a searching pair of eyes. It was a slightly peculiar-looking man, dressed plainly but respectably. She instinctively linked arms with the doctor and pulled her away with her; eventually, the follower's footsteps faded away. But soon thereafter, Minotschka heard them again. They seemed to occasion the doctor's uneasiness as well, for she pulled her companion from one side of the street to the other. A certain anxiety caught hold of the two women, they stopped talking to each other and hastened ahead. Once they arrived in front of her house, Minotschka took out her house keys and looked up the street, where she again spied their pursuer. But before she could express anything to the other woman, the doctor said: "Oh, please allow me to come upstairs

---

1 First published in 1886, Krafft-Ebing's *Psychopathia Sexualis* was one of the first sexological texts to discuss and frame as pathological non-normative sexual behaviors and identities. The book had a profound effect on late-nineteenth- and twentieth-century attitudes toward homosexuality.

with you for a moment, I believe I have torn my hem and would like to sew it up first."

Upstairs the doctor, noticeably anxious, rushed to the window. She mechanically fiddled about her dress, even though the student's sharp eyes saw that her late-night visitor's clothes were not at all torn. Only after quite a while did the doctor decide to leave.

Minotschka watched her from her window and noticed that the man was still down there and following Tatjana. "It must be some impertinent rogue," she thought out loud, but deep down, this experience troubled her and she kept pondering it for a long time.

When she stepped toward her desk, she saw a letter lying on it: it bore the countess's handwriting! Immediately the student forgot Tatjana and her unpleasant pursuer. Yet the letter contained only a few lines. Marta let her know that her father had recovered and gone home, and that she would reach Geneva in the next few days.

"Thank God, now I am safe from all temptation!" she muttered. She instinctively felt that her relationship with Pierette was growing more and more intimate every day, and that in the long run it would not work out the way she had hoped for early on.

True to her word, the countess arrived by the given train, and Minotschka, full of heartfelt joy, accompanied her to the small villa. They had such an endless number of things to tell each other, and also so many lost hours of togetherness to make up, that the time just flew.

Both of them had eagerly taken up their studies again, and there were only relatively minor events interrupting the monotony of their work. Minotschka had invited her companions for the Christmas celebration, Berta Cohn returned the favour on the 26th, and New Year's Eve was spent in delicious festivity at the Polish woman's house. A short time later, they celebrated the Russian New Year at Boris's, and a bit thereafter, for her birthday apparently, made merry at Tatjana's. The week passed quickly, Mardi Gras was around the corner, all of Geneva lived and breathed in the delirium of carnival season. On one of those days, following Minotschka's advice, the small circle of friends had planned on attending a masked ball, less for the entertainment than because Minotschka, in a fit of self-torture, wanted to throw herself into the follies of everyday people.

Then on the morning of that day, the countess arrived at the student's place. She seemed agitated and exhausted, very different from usual. "What's wrong?" Minotschka asked, worried.[1]

"Read this!" she said, instead of answering, holding a letter out to her friend. Hastily she skimmed the few lines, which announcing Marta's father's sudden death, bade her come to Warsaw immediately. "Dear God," Minotschka stammered. "Poor Marta!" Timidly, she put her arm around her friend's shoulder and embraced her. "Poor Marta," she said again. "Do you really want to leave?"

"Of course!" she replied, without losing her countenance for even a moment. "I am leaving, Minotschka, and I know that difficult weeks lie ahead of me. Also, I shall hardly be able to return this semester. Nothing of this would disquiet me, if it weren't for the thought that I need be deprived of you for so long! Tell me, darling, will you still hold me dear until I return?"

Then Minotschka knelt down in front of the Polish woman and pressed her closely. All she felt was unspeakable bliss, since nothing more mattered to her friend than the fact that she would have to part from her. "I will await your return, and until then, I shall only half live," she said. "Don't forget that, and come back as soon as you can!"——

A few days later the countess departed, after Minotschka had given her word that she would await her return, no matter how long it would take.

The days passed far too quickly for the student: before the semester's end, there was still so much to review that the changeable events of this last half year had impeded. Minotschka missed none of her lectures, and until late into the night she poured over her books, which alone offered her diversion in the dreary time of Marta's absence.

Then one afternoon Berta Cohn burst quite unexpectedly into her room. "Have you already heard? Have you already heard?"

"What?" Minotschka asked with little interest.

"Tatjana Kassberg fled last night, literally fled, since she probably would have been arrested!"

"But why! For heaven's sake, why?" Minotschka asked incredulously.

"Oh, it's a terrible story!" said the Jewess, throwing herself into an armchair. "First, though, please give me a cognac." After receiving the desired refreshment, she hastily recounted: "Last

---

1   This is the first moment in the text where the two women use the intimate *du* to address each other.

night Tatjana was as usual—*du jour*—in the clinic; she and the resident physician, who has now taken over her earlier position, were sharing the night shift. Then she heard a relatively loud exchange with the porter in the staircase hall below. Tatjana crept to the stairs and leaned over the banister. And after listening for a while, she stormed past her astonished colleague, down a long, dark hallway, into the operating room, and from there, probably to the small stairway leading to the maternity ward, and then she likely reached the street via the other gate. In short, they were detectives who spoke with the porter, and they wanted to arrest Tatjana. They had already been following and watching her for some time, because of certain political activities. In any event, Tatjana has fortunately escaped, as she has returned neither to her apartment nor to any of her acquaintances."

"Is it even possible!" stammered Minotschka, and lightning quick the scene arose in front of her: that strange man who had followed her and Tatjana. Even then doubts had arisen in her, though she had not wanted to admit as much, that she had suspected the man of being a detective. "The poor woman," she murmured, distraught. "The poor woman! But why not send a message to Mischah?" she added. "After all, he's her cousin; surely he'll know, what all of this means!"

"Just wait," laughed the Jewess. "That's already been done! But when they arrived at his apartment, the dear cousin had also disappeared without a trace, and apart from those two, two other Russian female students and two Russian male students."

"Dear, oh dear," murmured Minotschka while striding up and down the room in agitation. As she did so, she whistled "The Red Sarafan"[1] through her teeth. "This is awful!" she continued. "But what does Boris say to this? Haven't you already spoken with him?"

Before the Jewess could answer, there was a knock on the door, which simultaneously opened. It was Boris. "Minotschka Fernandowna," he called out just as he entered. "What do you say to Tatjana and all the others? An entire clandestine press was discovered where they live. They were producing a nihilist newspaper, which they were sending to Russia. Almost all local Russians are suspected, guilty or not! Isn't that madness!"[2]

---

1   Russian folksong composed by Aleksandr Varlamov (1801–48); libretto by Nikolay Tsyganov (1797–1831).

2   The reference here to Russian radical political engagement has its basis in fact. In 1873, alarmed by Russian women students' political activity at the University of Zurich, Tsar Alexander II (r. 1855–81) in effect forced them to leave.

"Yes, it's completely terrible!" said Minotschka, "but what to do?"

"That is precisely why I've come to you," said Boris; "the Russian consul is after all a cousin of your father! Please do me the favour of inquiring privately what all of this means. As a Frenchwoman you can do so without incurring any risk!"

Minotschka was immediately prepared to do so, and with the promise to give Boris an answer as soon as that evening, she went to call on her Russian relative. He, however, neither wanted to give any further details nor could he, and he only assured her that the guilty had all either fled or been taken into custody, and that the others would face no danger or suspicion. Minotschka sighed with relief, since apart from Boris she still had many good acquaintances that were part of the Russian colony. What had become of the dentist, no one could say. She had not been seen, not even several days before Mischah's escape.

Slowly the agitated souls calmed themselves. Everything returned to the right track. Since Marta's departure, Pierette had completely attached herself to Minotschka. And even if she had consciously assumed a certain responsibility for the other woman's future and saw certain things in the child that perplexed her, Minotschka felt more and more that Pierette was offering her far more than friendship alone. On the one hand, Minotschka did not have the courage to clarify her own situation to the actress; on the other hand, Marta's delayed return had embittered her and perhaps even rendered her a bit defiant. She did not know whether in the long run she could resist the temptation of the love that was being offered her. She also cared for Pierette far too much to have it come to an abrupt end. Amidst all these disturbances and developments the semester neared its close; no one worked with the same zeal anymore; one professor after another suspended his lectures; and one day Minotschka explained that there was no longer any purpose to remain in Geneva. After a merry farewell party, she departed in the company of the actress and with Boris, who also wanted to go to Munich for the following semester.

The three arrived in Munich only in mid-October. For some time Minotschka had felt strangely preoccupied; a wild impetuousness had overtaken her, making it impossible for her to stay in any place for long. The autumn days were exceptionally beautiful and warm and so she had proposed to her two companions that, before they resumed their work, they take a detour from

Switzerland in order to visit the Bavarian royal castles.[1] They stopped everywhere one or two days, entirely according to their fancy, and had then arrived in Traunstein. Here Minotschka vowed not to turn around until she had seen Salzburg; she absolutely had to spend one of those famous evenings on Gaisberg Mountain. And so they arrived in Salzburg, visited the fortress, the monasteries, the churches, and the interesting churchyard,[2] and every evening on Gaisberg listened to a military band, and still Minotschka wanted to hear nothing about a departure. She felt so peculiar, as if she had to make haste to reclaim yet more delightful hours, as if she would be approaching something dreadful, when she travelled to Munich. "My goodness," she said to her two companions, "how terribly foolish people are; they deprive themselves of everything and horde all that's beautiful for old age, for a time that they actually have no idea whether they'll live to see! But even if they experience it, it can only bring them disappointment, for man becomes dull and incapable of enjoyment; and he also no longer desires as much. What we have yearned for also matters less, when we obtain it when we are old, for only the eyes of youth see everything in a fairytale light. Savour the hour," she continued fervently, "so that we won't resemble those people who only wear their finery a few times a year for holidays, and the rest of the time consign it to moths and dust!"

Then she laughed and drank to divine frivolity. And so each day gave way to the next. Finally, she wanted to depart; stubbornly she claimed that the drunken farmers whom they had by chance encountered had spoiled her taste for Salzburg; that she could no longer stand the noise of the wooden clogs in front of the hotel; and that Austrian food would give her stomach-catarrh. She put forward the most nonsensical things in order to make excuses for herself: for she knew she was fleeing a ghost that would nonetheless eventually overtake her.

Hardly had they reached Munich when Minotschka regained her old drive and energy. She rented two rooms on Giselastrasse

---

1   Likely the castles of Linderhof, Hohenschwangau, Neuschwanstein, and Herrenchiemsee, which are all linked to King Ludwig II of Bavaria (r. 1864–86).
2   The Salzburger Kirchhof or churchyard was perhaps known to Minotschka because of the poem of the same name, written by Nikolaus Lenau (1802–50).

and found accommodations for the little actress on Maximiliansplatz; Boris had found lodging in Schwabing.[1] Then Minotschka left off advertisements for Pierette at various newspapers and made the necessary visits to university professors.[2] Already within fourteen days Pierette had four students, and within another fourteen, an afternoon position with a professor's family, so that for the time being she could be free from worry. Minotschka did not pass that much time in the company of her charge; she avoided meeting her as much as possible, for now gratitude had joined Pierette's hitherto existing love, and the little one had developed such an obstinate passion that Minotschka was left truly concerned for her. She had neither time nor interest in any flirtation, and the great, powerful love for Marta Kinzey still fulfilled her entire being. The latter had written her another long letter, followed now and then by a cursory card. Then another three weeks passed without hearing any news from the Polish woman, and Minotschka hoped that this might be connected to her unexpected arrival. But then one day a letter arrived once again; Marta wrote in detail of how much the pain of losing her father had affected her; how much responsibility and burden rested on her as the only child; that she had two capable managers but that she nonetheless would not be able to leave before the end of harvest time; moreover she felt so assailed that she did not think that she would come to Munich that summer. Before then she would go to a spa on the North Sea; Helgoland or Sylt were in consideration.[3] Minotschka should shorten her semester and go with her; were that not possible, they would then certainly meet in Munich the following winter.

Despite her heartfelt greetings and ample protestations of her yearning, Minotschka experienced feelings of disappointment and emptiness. Her friend's letter truly disturbed her and caused her the greatest disquiet. She reprimanded herself for her foolishness, she who until then had detested any sentimentality. But

---

1 In German, *Strasse* is street and *Platz* is square. *Maximiliansplatz* is in the city center. *Giselastrasse* is about a 30-minute walk away and is located in the bohemian *Schwabing* district, near the university. In the mid-1890s, Adelt-Duc herself lived on *Giselastrasse*.

2 Women's formal enrollment at the University of Munich was not permitted until 1903. Women could, however, audit courses.

3 Helgoland consists of two islands in the North Sea; Sylt is the largest German island in the North Sea. Both are known for their resorts.

the evil feeling of doubt came again and again, no matter how forcefully she threw herself into her work. In order not to be alone with Pierette too often, she had quite attached herself to Boris. The little one was very content with her work, and had blossomed into a completely different, happy creature. In October she was to move in with the professor's family and serve solely as the children's governess. This fact had led Minotschka to a certain impasse and a certain peace; she felt relieved of further responsibility. Pierette had however refused to accept readily the offer the professor's family had made. She did not wish to stay in Munich, were Minotschka not to remain in Munich, and she wanted a promise from her friend that she would see her often. Minotschka promised the little one as much, though a sacrifice attended this assurance: she would continue to remain in Munich, even though she had reached the decision to go to Berlin, for she no longer doubted that Marta Kinzey would still come to her.

In her unhappy mood she had allowed herself to be misled and to join a bowling club; through Boris she had made countless Russian acquaintances; she also frequently visited a Russian couple, Herr and Frau Tarpolsky, who often invited her for the evening; conviviality and distraction were not lacking. At one point at tea Nadine Tarpolsky turned the conversation to Tatjana Kassberg; and so to her great astonishment Minotschka discovered that after her escape from Geneva the doctor had spent four weeks with the couple in Munich; Mischah and the dentist had also appeared, though after two days they had departed ahead of her for Russia. Even so, the Tarpolskys would not and could not say anything further about Tatjana and her escape. Minotschka detected their fear of betraying themselves in anything, whether in words or looks, especially when the couple had other Russian guests.

Once again, she frequently undertook bicycle tours, and as a result learned of a cycling club comprised of two Baronesses von Blum, a painter, several women painters, and a law student. All of the female members were independent women who openly confessed to being members of the third sex. And with them Minotschka engaged her favourite topic with renewed zeal. Often of an evening they would frequent the Löwenbräu-Keller,[1] where, accompanied by magnificent beer and the sound of music, the small group engaged in serious conversations. And so they came

---

1 A famous Munich pub, featuring, of course, *Löwenbräu* beer.

to talk about the condition of women in Germany, their oppression and the barriers imposed on their thirst for knowledge. Nadine, who had also studied, recounted much regarding her experiences, and in the end let herself be tempted to assert that she certainly believed that German women were less capable of entering a scientific profession than any other women of any nation. "I don't believe that!" Minotschka responded excitedly. "For taking into account today's successes and the tireless advance of female reformers for women's progress, we must needs be amazed, filled with respectful astonishment, that German women across all generations have preserved such a high degree of intelligence as to be able to undertake the difficult fight for knowledge and the freedom to pursue any profession. What with the mental starvation diet to which they have been subjected, we must wonder that they haven't become idiots and intellectual cretins. In this case, despite her apparent lagging behind, a woman is actually far ahead of a man, whom no one hinders, when he wants to satiate his intellectual hunger. A woman, though, stands in front of a gate, and, until now, only determined, hardy natures have succeeded in climbing the high gate in order to nurse their intellectual hunger beyond the barrier."

"Certainly," opined Herr Tarpolsky, "women are tenacious and intelligent, and I believe that some men in good positions are unable, in the matter of intelligence, to measure up to any great number of uneducated women, since it is not education and knowledge alone but rather, first and foremost, intelligence that distinguishes a person. For this reason, whether regarding a man or a woman, one should recognise this: intelligence should be developed, cared for, expanded; only a free, acute intelligence will lead to a genuine elevation of intellectual character. Look around in our masculine circles, and you will be astonished how many learned men you will find whose education has been one-dimensional. They are all people who, lacking in any true intelligence, are committed to petty, narrow-minded attitudes. One finds intelligence, however, as I have already emphasised, in both sexes to the same degree, only it is nurtured quite differently!"

"But," said the Russian stranger in attendance, "though I hold the female and male sexes to be absolutely equal with regard to intelligence, I believe that women are still in some respects more frivolous, less reliable, and more flighty. Don't you know the lovely Russian saying," he jested, "What is lighter than a feather? Dust! And what is lighter than dust? The wind! And what is lighter than the wind? Woman!?"

"Aha," Minotschka laughed, "you are forgetting something, my dear sir, because then comes the addendum. And what's lighter than woman? Man!"

Everyone laughed. "These are little jests," the stranger said, "yet I nonetheless believe that no matter how things will develop in life women will always be in some respects subordinate to men! These are after all the laws of nature, which reach their zenith in nature. A woman needs a man if only in order to ensure progeny."

"My heavens, yes," said Dr. Tarpolsky, "this is all very clear and logical, dear friend; but that is not to say that every woman after she has borne one or more children would wish to remain in any sort of sexual relationship with the man. Certainly we have to have men and women of normal feelings in order to maintain the world properly; but that doesn't give the state the right to saddle all of us with the duty of marrying!"

"But you are married," laughed the former speaker. "But only in our own way," said Tarpolsky evasively.

And in that moment Minotschka knew that the two were not bound together by any legal bond.

"I am not for free love," Tarpolsky continued, "but I am against marriage, which chains two people together for life, without knowing if they will always be enough for each other, for the falsest fairytale is the fairytale of eternal love! Health and material concerns play far too an important role in people's lives, for any affinity to be maintained forever. Spiritual bonds can of course tie two people together, though they, too, over time only lose their hold. For even in the best marriage a certain spiritual void, an emotional alienation takes hold, as soon as the sexual relationship between the man and the woman has, more or less, spent itself. One becomes critical, in one's regard and observation, once the first love-madness has passed. One sees in the not-beloved attributes and vices that transform love into indifference and disgust or hatred, attributes that deeply offend our aesthetic sensibility. On this crisis in married life marriage founders or fastens itself: either cohabitation becomes intolerable and the possibility to be able to dissolve the bond must needs exist or one arrives at a kind of friendship, a kind of protective and offensive alliance for the benefit of the state; one stays together, and ... loves elsewhere!"

"Yes," said Minotschka, "and marital friendship can sometimes also be valuable and lead to a comfortable, peaceful monotony that knows no tempestuous illusion, nor the desperate jealousy of love! One adapts to the other half and in this way manages well enough. If peace already passes as a marital achievement, then that's proof thereof, that marriage is a period of storm and stress, whose best victory is truce!"

"My heavens, yes!" said the stranger. "You are quite right! For, after all, love does not exist in the marital picture that is painted for us. Love is only beautiful in its inception and development! The first stage of maturation already brings decay, and the death of love is the most hideous of deaths."

Suddenly an idea coursed through Minotschka's thoughts. "What do you think of fidelity?" she asked expectantly.

"Fidelity, fidelity," the earlier speaker considered, "fidelity is after all only an abstraction! It has two sides: on the one side, it is an intentional expression of the person, a self-castigation that is, however, quite harmless; on the other side, it is more dangerous, a compulsion, an imposed abstraction that one should not refuse to unveil."

"So something purely individual, desired, and personal?" Minotschka asked.

"Certainly," he replied: "Of all feelings it's the most personal!"

"And do you think that one cannot consequently be held responsible for a breach of faith?" she persisted.

"No, of course not," he replied, "that's included in what I said before!"

A thoughtful silence followed; and since Minotschka and the Russian stranger, who had until now directed the principal conversation, hardly exchanged a word more, they soon dispersed in an imperceptible ill humour.

The semester ever more neared its close. For a long time Minotschka had had no sign of life from the Polish woman; finally today she received a letter, which had however been hastily and carelessly composed. Marta spoke endlessly of Sylt, where she was now sojourning, and of her surroundings. An ailing officer, unbelievably musical, reappeared in all of her sentences, next to lengthy discussions of music. She related in precise detail how she played this or that fugue and how the officer in question did. She hardly spoke of herself and Minotschka! A few despairing assurances of love followed only at the end, but they, however, despite their liveliness, seemed contrived. A dull apathy overpowered Minotschka; she apprehended a sort of doom, and she also knew that this doom could

only be connected to Marta. This letter had in every way strengthened her mistrust, and even now she felt a feeling of hatred for this unknown officer! She saw him as a foe; instinctively she recognised him as such.——
For the Catholic population of Munich, Assumption Day is an important holiday that is also publically observed.[1] Universities were closed, and already the previous day, Minotschka and Boris had decided that, since the weather was glorious, they would undertake a longer cycling excursion on the holiday. There had been a thunderstorm the night before; the air was cool and wonderfully fragrant. A delicate mist overspread the early-morning midsummer landscape. The country road looked as if freshly washed. Birds sang gaily in the forest, and overhead the sun lay hidden behind the clouds, only at times appearing, like a furtive smile from the heavens. The two cyclists were both accustomed to the heat; besides, the country road was smooth and in excellent condition. They glided along on their bicycles, as if floating. They took their breakfast in a tavern hidden in the woods, sitting at plain wooden tables underneath the fir trees, and in the afternoon, on their return, they had their coffee by a small, dark lake. Dusk had already fallen when they reached Munich again; the steeples of the Frauenkirche were barely visible. Boris accompanied Minotschka to her apartment; they only wanted to put up their bicycles and then spend the evening in the Löwenbräu beer garden. Awaiting Minotschka at home were some letters, which she wanted to read directly. She skimmed the first two with indifference, when she suddenly started at the sight of the third.... It was the Polish woman's handwriting! She opened the letter; four densely written pages stared back at her; she sat down close to the lamp, around which several large moths were circling. She read.... A strange, gurgling sound escaped her; then she turned over the letter that she had read, and read it through again. As she did so, her features changed, and suddenly, as if numb, she let the paper slide from her hand. She sat motionless in her chair, absentmindedly, but then, with a sudden scream, she buried her face in her hands and burst into wild, desperate sobs. Boris was completely speechless; he had never seen a person cry in this manner, with such a whimpering, terrified, painful sound! He leapt toward her and pulled her up.

---

1   The Feast of the Assumption is celebrated on 15 August.

"Minotschka Fernandowna!" he cried out in horror. "What is the matter?" But she was lifeless, as if her body were present but her mind far away. He spoke in a pleading, consoling, and reproachful manner, but she did not seem to understand. Gradually, she ceased crying. The letter lay at her feet on the carpet and she kept peering down at it, as if it were something that fascinated her. Boris, in heartfelt terror, had filled a glass with wine and offered her it. She did not however move; so he lifted it up to her lips, and mechanically she drank it all. She looked around the room, her gaze fixed and vacant, as if looking for help. Then, with a strange expression in her eyes, as if she had to remember where she was, she looked up at Boris. She rose to her feet, but staggered! Boris caught her in his arms; and then she instinctively put her arms around his neck, as her head fell heavily onto his shoulder. He felt the severe, convulsing tremors of her body.

"Minotschka," he pleaded over and over again, "what is the matter with you? Please tell me what is tormenting you; I am so very concerned for your well-being!" After a while, she lifted herself up, and with a sad attempt at a smile, looked at her friend. He was horrified at her expression; her face was so very strange, her features entirely changed! And then, in a daze, she groped for the letter. Slowly, she tore it into countless little pieces and carelessly let them drop to the floor; they lay on the carpet like white snowflakes. As she stood motionless in the same spot, Boris handed her another glass of wine; this time she took it and emptied it slowly, deliberately. All of a sudden, she reached for her hat and gloves and, turning to Boris, only said: "Come!" He was glad that they could leave the cramped room, for he hoped that the necessity of maintaining her composure in the presence of strangers would more readily allow Minotschka to come to her senses. She clung heavily to his arm and pulled him along with her. Without speaking she dragged him up and down the streets. Sometimes they walked in circles and turned again into the same street through which they had just passed. She apparently didn't know where she was, she only kept staring ahead with large, burning eyes.

"Are you looking for something, Minotschka?" he lovingly asked her after a while. She only shook her head no, and this strange walk continued onward, into the narrow, crooked lanes of Munich, into the less respectable neighbourhoods. Now music could be heard; it was a music-hall melody, bubbly and sweet, invigorating and seductive. Minotschka steered them toward the establishment over whose entrance a large, blood-red lantern hung. It was as if it drew her on! "Let's go inside!" she said imperiously, letting go of Boris's arm.

"But good heavens, Minotschka!" he pleaded. "We cannot possibly go inside! I will escort you anywhere, wherever you wish; just not in there!" But she had already begun to step toward the entrance on her own and to place her hand on the doorknob; Boris rushed to stay by her side.

The establishment was a café-chantant[1] of the lowest rung. To the back of the small, smoke-filled room, there was a stage-like construction on which a troupe of provocatively and fantastically dressed singers sat. On the platform in front stood one of the women, who, in a quite pitiful dress, with skirts gathered high, shouted out that vulgar tune, whose bubbly melody they had heard outside. With every refrain, the guests cheered and hollered, and sang along. All the guests were men. They eyed the arriving couple with surprise, but since they were obviously foreigners, it was assumed that they had only entered the establishment out of ignorance of its character. They sat down in a quiet corner; Minotschka stared fixedly at the screeching singer, as if with great interest. Apparently she neither heard the singing, nor perceived the dubious nature of the establishment. They sat like this for a long time! Minotschka drank the cool, dark beer mechanically, as if with a feverish thirst. Suddenly, however, she jumped to her feet and rushed past the startled Boris. The latter paid quickly and rushed after her. He found her on the street in front of the establishment: she was leaning against a wall and pressing her hands to her face; again, a wild, convulsive sobbing shook her body. Quietly he pulled her away. He placed her arm on his and led her down the street, but said nothing to her. Her tears had dried again. "Take me home!" she said suddenly. "But quickly, quickly; I want to get home as soon as possible!"

When they arrived at her house, Boris pleaded with her to let him come upstairs and stay with her. But impatiently and vigorously she deterred him! "Oh please, please, Minotschka!" he said. "I cannot leave you alone, I am so very worried about you!"——

"Leave," she commanded brusquely, as she moved toward the hallway.

"Minotschka," he begged, seizing her hand, "Minotschka, just promise me this! You are not going to harm yourself, are you?"

---

1 A café that offers musical entertainment.

Then, once again, she looked at him with a calm expression of recognition. Her voice had regained some of its earlier firmness, as she said, with contempt: "Of course not!"

Still Boris could not bring himself to leave his friend to her fate. He fearfully paced up and down beneath her windows; but these stayed open and no light could be seen in her room. Probably Minotschka, in her pain, had thrown herself fully dressed onto the bed and was fast asleep! Only as dawn broke did Boris return to his apartment.

For four weeks, Minotschka remained unavailable to anyone; even her intimates were turned away by the landlady, at the express wishes of her tenant. The student was seen neither at club meetings nor at university; she also did not dine at their favourite restaurant. Even those friends who, full of concern, lingered near her house and kept watch, did not have any opportunity to meet her. She was apparently not leaving her room! It was said that she was writing a scientific paper and did not wish to be disturbed. And when finally her companions were allowed to call on her again, they found her buried under writings and piles of old bulky folios.——

They were used to her strange behaviour, and so they let her be. And yet, the friends were also intimidated by the brusque manner with which Minotschka had on earlier occasions met any caring inquiries.

One evening she appeared at the club, unexpectedly: she greeted everyone as if nothing had ever happened. Not even the sharpest eye could detect any change in her personality; perhaps at most she was a bit more harsh than usual. When everyone was gathered together, she tapped her glass, stood up, and announced in a loud, clear voice to her surprised audience: "My dear companions, I must inform you that our former member, the Countess Kinzey, will not be returning to our circle as one of us, neither in Geneva nor in Munich nor anywhere else! Six weeks ago she married an officer in Leipzig!"

For a while there was silence; then a storm broke loose; some were surprised, others appalled, perplexed. But as much as they wanted to learn more from Minotschka, she answered no further questions. When she had finished her announcement, her eyes met Boris's for an instant! ... In that very moment, he had understood the evening ...

Minotschka had sat down in the back of the room next to a law student with whom she appeared to be eagerly and passionately discussing the housing situation in Berlin. Her announcement regarding the countess now seemed incidental.

Minotschka only attended one more club meeting that semester. When vacation arrived, she went away by herself, without telling anyone where, only promising the actress that she would return to Munich. Nor did she prove any more social the next semester, so that they gradually began to leave her to herself. Moreover, Boris was nearing his doctoral examinations, and once he had passed, he left for home. He knew that Minotschka offered him no hope, and so he parted from her with the conviction that life would never again bring them together.——

Two years had passed. The circle of former university friends had scattered to the four winds. A few months before, the Viennese had moved to Bosnia, to be a doctor; Berta Cohn was working on her doctoral dissertation in Zurich; and the actress, having found an old, childless benefactress, who promised to provide for her future, was living as her companion in the South. Students coming from Russia reported that they had seen Tatjana Kassberg in St. Petersburg; she was not practicing as a physician but seemed to be a very prominent person in club activities there. She ostensibly planned to move with her friend, the man from Geneva, the one who had been exiled, and settle down in Siberia. Minotschka had not heard anything from the Polish woman for more than six months; she avoided any and all conversations and inquiries regarding Countess Kinzey; the wound was still painful. She herself had used up almost all of her capital and had therefore looked for permanent employment. That summer she was to travel to Australia, where she would assume oversight of an international training school in Sydney.[1] She knew that she would remain there for the rest of her life, and leaving Europe already felt like a partial death to her. She would most likely never be heard of again, and for her, too, it would hardly be likely to learn any news of her erstwhile acquaintances. She would encounter different circumstances, among different people, in a distant, foreign land—the unfathomable ocean separating her from all that had been, the joys and sorrows of her life! She was choosing voluntary exile! In the last while, she had

---

1   "Training school" is our translation of *Fortbildungsschule*, which, in a late-nineteenth-century German context, offered students occupational preparation, particularly with regard to industry. Technical colleges, by contrast, focused on preparation for individual branches of industry.

been overtaken by a boundless fatigue and hopelessness. Oft it seemed not worth her while to do battle with life on behalf of herself, for her advancement, for the years that, whether many or few, lay ahead of her, in which nothing of significance would be achieved. She felt detached from all human sentiments, as if she were entirely alone among living creatures who did not understand her, unknown, lost, forgotten within the infinitude of mankind! One year would follow another, always and ever the same, only bearing the certainty of having neared an unknown end, darkness, the unexplored!

And then, quite suddenly, a yearning for her homeland awoke within her, a burning, wild desire to see once more the haunts of her glorious childhood and youth. She was in a terrible hurry to escape cold Munich, and to spend sunny April days in Paris. A morbid avidity for French soil befell her, an unbridled fear that she would not be able to regain her homeland, her country. Now all those years she had lived abroad seemed like an agonising martyrdom; she could not understand how she could have ever been happy. She recalled the most unimportant and inconsequential people from her homeland, and, with an eager restlessness, anticipated addressing each with a kind word. She imagined herself so thoroughly in terms of the past, expecting to find everything unchanged, that she would hardly have been surprised to be treated like a little girl again. She travelled to Paris directly, without interruption. Such was her state of nervous agitation, she could not eat anything for two days.

And now more and more lights began to appear along the route. A dull, rushing sound could be heard, like the roar of a distant waterfall—the mighty pulsing of a vast city! The train rolled into the city, over the countless tracks and switches; a hissing, a jolt—they had arrived in Paris! Minotschka was trembling all over: she let her fellow travellers descend first. A dark mist covered her eyes; she barely reached the perron[1] and the exit. She went to the first available hotel. She would realise that she was in Paris, breathe in the city's air, and hear her mother tongue—then she would feel well and refreshed again! But how mistaken she was! Her infirmity increased, she managed with difficulty to swallow a few bites of the food she had been brought, then she sank into an armchair by the window. She stared down at the street, where pedestrians and vehicles rushed

---

1 A train platform; a platform at the top of one or two flights of stairs that is located at the entrance of a large building.

past in ceaseless motion, but her eyes could no longer take in the city scenery.

When she reawakened, or regained consciousness, she was shivering. It must have been very late, for the street was relatively quiet. For a time Minotschka stumbled about, then, she undressed without any light and lay down in bed. She had no clear idea of where she was, and she drifted off to sleep with the nagging question: "Am I in Geneva, Bern, or Munich?"

It was late by the time she awoke the next morning; she had forgotten to wind her watch, but the clock over on the Gare du Nord[1] indicated the hour. She felt well but not refreshed; the old restlessness had overtaken her once more and drove her out-doors. She drank coffee served in a glass and then rushed outside! Paris! Parisian soil! A feeling of sentimentality overcame her! She strolled down the Boulevard de Strasbourg, then turned right, walking along the boulevards in order to reach Boulevard Haussmann. She wished to go to Passy,[2] on foot, to the street where she had once lived! In her tomboyish clothing, the stranger was met with astonished looks as she passed by; she stood out twice as much in Paris, where people dressed ele-gantly. But she paid no attention! She continued on slowly and her gaze absorbed everything, everything seemed so familiar, so dear. An omnibus turned the corner just then. "Passy-Bonise," the indicated line! That was her route, her omnibus, the one that she as a child and young girl had ridden daily; the one that had faithfully carried her summer and winter. Her eyes moistened. And all of a sudden, she found that long-awaited feeling of hap-piness, protection; the feeling that all of these people belonged to her and spoke her language, that she was now home, in her homeland! A childlike rush of happiness took hold of her; she stopped everywhere, here to buy a small bouquet from a flower vendor and there a paper from a newsboy. It seemed as if every single person knew her from before, as if every polite "Merci, madame" were thanking her for having returned.

She called out to a fiacre[3] and told the driver to take her slowly to Passy, along the Seine and then over to the Eiffel Tower. She wanted to take her breakfast there and felt a sudden hunger. Everywhere around her there were gaily dressed people,

---

1   One of Paris's large railway stations. The station name is misspelled in the original text.

2   An area of Paris in the 16th *arrondissement*, on the Rive Droite.

3   A small, four-wheeled carriage for hire; a hackney-coach; a French cab.

flowers upon flowers on every corner and street, and the scent of blooming chestnut trees in warm sunlight—the incomparable beauty of April days in Paris! She took in the bustle, which so easily invites gaiety, and then it struck her that in a few weeks, the ocean would separate her from this bit of land, her home! A searing pain tore through her—then she lifted herself up and shouted with sudden relief, in German: "I will not go to Sydney, no, I will certainly not go to Sydney!" The driver turned around: "Madame désire?"[1] he asked.

"Oh, rien, rien!"[2] she laughed giddily. She breathed a sigh of relief, as if a heavy burden had been lifted from her heart, as if she had escaped a terrible fate. "I will not go, I will not go," she continued to murmur, but now laughing, happy, saved!

She had briefly beheld her former childhood home on the Rue de Passy: now there was so much time for that, since she would remain at home, in Paris after all! After paying the driver, she went up to the second story of the Eiffel Tower. She felt a youthful hunger, as she had during her school years! The food, bread, wine of home! Drunk with joy she gazed down at the blessed, blossoming land, at the elegant, large city with the Seine as its silver belt! One could follow its course far up and clearly see the small island near Asnières, and then down to the banks toward Meudon. A sweet fragrance rose from below, where the first, lush spring grass was being mown. "Oh my homeland," said the young woman, "how could I have ever considered leaving you forever!" Ecstatic, she tore her boater from her head, and the boisterousness of her student years came over her as she waved it in a greeting to the city, and joyfully shouted: "Veni, vidi, vici![3] You have me now; keep me here!"——

She had already been in Paris eight days without even having thought about finding employment. She had sent a long cable to Sydney, followed by an explanatory letter. Let them see where they could find "a French headmistress with excellent language skills"! She, Minotschka Fernandoff, would stay in Paris! During the day she went for walks. She had been to all of her favourite places, the charming spots along the Seine, in Versailles, in St. Germain. She had found the large meadow and the old building-site in Passy unchanged, why, even the old woman who sold

---

1 French: Madame wishes?
2 French: Oh, nothing, nothing!
3 Latin: I came, I saw, I conquered (Julius Caesar's famous pronouncement of victory).

chestnuts in front of the Trocadéro[1] still remembered her! And yet ten years had passed, and she wasn't any longer an enthusiastic young girl, but a serious, experienced woman, mature, at twenty-eight, as only women who are engaged in intellectual work are.——

Today she was to visit Père Lachaise.[2] She went on foot; mindful that she was standing on Parisian cobblestones, she felt the need to walk quite a lot. On the Place de la République, she purchased some white daisies from a woman. She bought the flowers not really knowing what she was doing, but merely because the vendor had offered them to her. She looked down at the large, white spring starflowers——. A shadow fell over her face.——These were Marta Kinzey's favourite flowers, which she had kept in her room season after season and which she always wore in a small bouquet in her belt. Minotschka saw the noble, quiet face of the Polish woman before her——. She saw herself in Leipzig with her friend, on their morning walks through Rosenthal Park. Once more she relived those days of their first acquaintance, when she had waited for hours under the window of the woman she adored, without finding the courage to go to her. And then, the Pentecost[3] holidays, there was the trip to Thuringia, where their hearts found each other, where they belonged to each other entirely, free and without restraint. What a lovely time they had had together in Geneva, working and striving together, in untroubled togetherness! And later, that dreadful day, when she learned of her friend's marriage ... Minotschka heard again in her ears the music-hall tune from that day; she clearly saw tall Boris in front of her, as if she could touch him.... But, no, anything but that, anything but to be reminded of those days, just now, when she needed to steady herself, and to settle the account of those foolish years of her youth!

Now she was standing in front of the entry gate to the city of the dead. She aimlessly turned from the main driveway into the small side paths. She barely encountered any other visitors. In

---

1 A palace built for the 1878 Universal Exhibition. It was demolished in 1937 and replaced by the Palais Chaillot. Today, the name refers to the grounds on which the Trocadéro Palace stood.
2 A famous Parisian cemetery.
3 Also known as Whitsunday, the seventh Sunday after Easter. The observance commemorates the appearance of the Holy Spirit among Jesus' disciples.

the days of budding spring and sunshine, few people take the time to think of the dead.

She left the main roads with their ostentatious monuments, their villa-like structures that suffocate the dead, as if the living feared their return. She visited the poor, simple graves, the resting sites of those who make no boast to death. Everywhere here, colourful flowers grew rank in careless abundance, painting dreary death with a merry face. It was peaceful here, beautiful and quiet. Then a lady turned at the crossing; undecided, she hesitated for a moment, then walked down the road in the same direction as Minotschka. The stranger wore mourning clothes, though mourning clothes that, suggesting a certain joy, evinced any number of emotions rather than sorrow. And with a feeling of mocking bitterness, Minotschka thought to herself that no other dress in the world allowed its wearer as much piquant coquettishness as did a certain type of mourning dress. The woman walking ahead of her wore a light, black dress made of silk crèpe, which she gathered up gracefully, and which displayed a mixture of lace, ruffles, and ruches. The black jet ornamentation of her hat sparkled in the sun, and her parasol looked like a large bouquet of black roses and lace. The stranger wore her blonde hair in thick, short curls, and——"Marta," murmured Minotschka involuntarily. Her blood rushed to her heart: that was the gait, the figure, the bearing of the countess, and most of all, the hair, her extraordinary blonde hair! For a second, she hesitated—it was as if she should hasten after the stranger and look at her face; then she turned decisively onto a side path. Was she suffering from hallucinations today, that she saw her lost friend everywhere and in everything? For so long now she had lulled herself into a seeming forgetfulness, and now everything reawakened at such an inopportune time, now that she was to start a new life! Why had she bought those alluring daisies, it was all their fault, they had turned her thoughts back toward the past and awakened her memories! A dilapidated, ill-kept grave stood off to the side. A mass of wild violets grew in abundance amidst the periwinkles and the light green spring grass. With a quick movement, Minotschka put the flowers down onto the stranger's grave. "Only peace, peace," she murmured. "It is better than happiness!" She stood motionless in front of the colorful mound for a long time; with effort she returned to reality. The air was fragrant and heavy; everywhere a buzzing and humming, characteristic of that gallant, spring,—the clouds moved hurriedly along at a dizzying height—and she herself was so tired, so tired and pleasantly exhausted!

She walked a few steps more to the next bench. How good it felt to take some rest! There was a crunch of gravel and a rustle of a woman's silk dress.—Minotschka looked up. There she was again, the stranger, she was approaching her ... And suddenly, with a scream, the lady in black sank down at Minotschka's feet. She embraced the motionless woman and suppressing a sob, murmured absent-mindedly, hoarsely, silently, "Minotschka, Minotschka!" The latter then shook off the feeling of numbness that had overtaken her, and pushing the kneeling woman back by her shoulders, she fervently asked: "Marta, Marta, is it really you?" The other woman raised her eyes. A world of pain and love shone from them, gazing at Minotschka. "How did you get here, how on earth did you get here?" the latter asked, doubtfully. "And where, where is—your husband?" She uttered the words with difficulty; gathering her thoughts cost her exertion. "But he is dead," Marta said. "He has been dead this half year! He was buried back in Davos! Since then, I have been wandering, without plan or purpose! I had not given up hope of finding you somewhere, even though I would not have dared to call on you! Milaya Minotschka, will you forgive me?"

But she received no reply. With a peculiar fixed gaze, Minotschka looked away from the questioning woman and stared at the countless gravesites.

"Please listen to me, Minotschka," pleaded the Polish woman. "Don't be so apathetic! You must see, I have never forgotten you, here with the dead as my witnesses I swear to you: I have never been more than a friend to my husband! It was music that brought us together! He knew everything, and he still wanted me to be his wife for the outside world; he wanted to be my companion in comradeship! Oh, Minotschka, oh how I suffered despite his love and goodness, and how horrible was fate's revenge for me—for you, if you'd like! No, our kind of woman must not marry, not even in friendship; it is against nature! Such a marriage is a poor, indefinable bond, a fetter, a violation, a sacrilege, at very least an unbearable burden! Oh, you have no idea how I have suffered! And you, you who are just and firm, do you wish now to judge me? Can you not forgive me? Can't you let the past be?"

Fearfully, she pressed Minotschka's hands.

"I am terrified," replied the latter in a dull voice. "I am terrified of a second disappointment! I no longer have any faith or trust!"

"But, Beloved," the Polish woman begged. "Beloved, be reasonable! Do not hide behind your pride, which will rob you of everything! Isn't it human to err? And did you not also err once? Will you condemn me, when I only offered a man friendship? Can't it be as it was before? You see, even spouses separate for a long time because of woeful misunderstandings, only, thereafter, to cleave to each other ever more firmly! Can't we do the same? Can't you overcome the past, can't you believe me anymore? Come with me to Warsaw, my estate is nearby. I will lead you around in the merry sunshine, through the golden cornfields! There, we shall complete each other; there you will be my beloved tyrant once more and I your obedient Marta. I shall attend your every wish and repent a thousand-fold anything that I have done to you in ignorance! And in the fall, we shall return here, to your homeland, which shall hold us fast until the warm sunshine beckons us anew to my region! Will you join me in this ever-changing flight; will you faithfully entrust me with your life? Minotschka, do you still love me?"——

Then Minotschka bent down, and pulling the kneeling woman up toward herself, said only: "I do!"

And so, arm in arm, they left, walking toward the city, out into the bliss of spring and the bliss of their life!

Appendix A: Reviews of Are They Women?

1. Review of *Sind es Frauen?*, *Westermanns Illustrierte Deutsche Monatshefte* [*Westermann's Illustrated German Monthly Magazine*] vol. 91, no. 2 (November 1901), p. 303

Taking a lesson from Wolzogen,[1] Frau Aimée Duc, a Frenchwoman, has written "A Novel Concerning the Third Sex": *Are They Women?*, a story set amidst female university student groups in Geneva and Munich. More discussion than novel but in many respects extremely instructive also pertaining to the theories of Elisabeth Dauthendey.[2]

2. From Numa Praetorius [Eugen Wilhelm], "Weibliche Homosexualität" ["Female Homosexuality"], *Jahrbuch für sexuelle Zwischenstufen* [*Yearbook for Intermediate Sexual Types*], vol. 5, no. 2 (1903), p. 1102

... The narrative's interest focuses on observations concerning the homosexual woman, marriage, and female emancipation on the whole, as well as on homosexual women's manner of thinking. One can only approve of the crux of these remarks, according to which the individuality of every woman should be developed, her abilities and needs taken into account, and only those women whose character and inclinations render them suitable should enter into marriage. The author strategically places her reflections on women's emancipation in the mouths of homosexual women—rightly so—given that their nature and their more masculine character, will undoubtedly be the most prototypical representatives of women's rights.

There is little substance to the narrative; nowhere are the themes and actions realised; the whole functions more as a sketch. The first part is almost exclusively comprised of interesting philosophical and socio-ethical discussions, while the second part contains the somewhat thin episodes of the denouement of the love relationship between Minotschka and the countess, as well as the portrayal of Minotschka's feelings of despair, desolation, and wistfulness, which the relationship's rupture calls forth in her soul.

---

1   Ernst von Wolzogen (1855–1934), author of *Das dritte Geschlecht* [*The Third Sex*] (1899).

2   Elisabeth Dauthendey (1854–1943), author of *Vom neuen Weibe und seiner Liebe* [*Regarding the New Woman and Her Love*] (1900).

Appendix B: Anita Augspurg on Women and Marriage

1. Anita Augspurg, "A Typical Case of the Present Time. An Open Letter" (1905)

[Anita Augspurg (1857–1943) was a German jurist, writer, and activist. A leading voice in the women's rights movement in the late nineteenth and early twentieth centuries, she also lived openly as a lesbian. Augspurg's essay "Ein typischer Fall der Gegenwart. Ein offener Brief" originally appeared in both *Die Frauenbewegung: Revue für die Interessen der Frauen* [*The Women's Movement: Journal for Women's Interests*], vol. 11, no. 11 (1905), pp. 81–82, and *Europa. Wochenschrift für Kultur und Politik* [*Europa. Culture and Politics Weekly*], vol. 1, no. 7 (1905), pp. 311–14.]

Dear Madam!

Your letter is the third within fourteen days to ask me for advice regarding the same matter. Rest assured, your letter's question has been taken up and seriously considered in our time not simply by three but in fact by a hundred of our nation's most able women. Therefore, please allow me to respond to you publically, so that my answer might possibly strengthen not only your resolve but also that of other women.

Your letter and the two others I have mentioned,—I receive such letters constantly; they are typical, as similar as leaves on a tree; they are a sign of the times. Out of your own strength and against familial wishes, you (and others) have created for yourself a fulfilling vocation, you enjoy an independent existence and your father's discontent has yielded to your success. You (and others) encountered a man—not at a ball or at any other occasion displaying the deceptive commotion of conviviality, but under simple and authentic circumstances; a man whose attitude toward life is as congenial to yours as it is contrary to the popular one. And one fine day and when your heart so moved you, but without notifying either friend or foe or eminent authority of your decision, you entered into a conjugal state with that man. Your happiness, which, by the way, you had guarded not with the apprehension stemming from a guilty conscience, but merely with the self-interest of wishing to remain undisturbed, did not stay hidden for long, and your family, mortally wounded in its societal honour, demands, at least through the lawful legitimisation of your marriage, an atonement for this affront. Your husband is willing to undertake this step, which for him only constitutes a meaningless convention; you have an instinctive feeling that dear philistine morality would exact more of you than a mere formality and something within you is resisting this sacrifice. Let it be said that the much vilified female instinct has most certainly hit the mark once again, since, for a woman, a legitimate marriage means the lawful renunciation of her legal existence. It includes not only the degrading relinquishment of her name and her right to self-determination, but in most cases complete pecuniary dependence and in all cases the total loss of any legal claim to her children.

For a self-respecting woman, who is aware of the lawful consequences of civil matrimony, it is thus impossible, I believe, to enter into a legitimate marriage: her drive for self-preservation, her respect for herself and her expectation of her husband's respect only leaves her with the possibility of a free union.[1]

In many, unfortunately actually in most, cases, pressing considerations regarding one's material existence render impossible a dignified assertion of one's personality. And in fact these considerations are almost more pressing for a man than for a woman, since women, who are still so rarely appointed to the civil service, most often need the free-lance professions much more, and in them they prove less dependent.[2] It is nearly impossible for a university lecturer, civil servant, or officer, to maintain his position if he openly lives in a free union; I fear that our legal and medical associations would reprimand their members for such behaviour. In this way, on average, a man's civil existence compels an enlightened modern woman to consciously sacrifice her own civil existence. But if there is any possibility for unconstrained independence and for enough personal self-confidence to defy philistine social proscription; if any woman dares also to raise her children so that they do not incommensurably suffer from those prejudices under whose curse they live and grow, then I consider it not only advisable, not only the right, but in fact the duty of the morally upstanding woman, to choose a free union and thus, by example, pave the way toward a more worthy formulation of marital laws than we

---

1 Augspurg uses the German term *freie Ehe*, which literally means free marriage. The English equivalent is free love or free union. Augspurg is referring to a marriage not contracted by or recognized under civil law.

2 Implicit in this sentence is a comparison between men's and women's professional opportunities: in contrast to men, women had little access to the civil service; in freelance professions (for example, teaching, journalism, midwifery, photography), women proved less dependent on access to a male-dominated hierarchy.

currently possess. It seems to me that only such propagandist action will lead to urgently needed legislative reforms.

You tell me, dear Madam, that your husband will never abuse his legal prerogative, "which he despises," and this is certainly the same conviction found among all those who are in the same situation as you. In one matter, however, he is not even able to negate the effects of legal matrimony, that is, the alteration of your name. Society continues to condemn protests regarding this point as a stubborn obsession with formalities. The imposition of suddenly abandoning the name under which one has matured into a human being and exchanging it for a new one, as if one were discarding a worn-out garment, is, however, far more than a mere formality. You only have to look at it objectively, in order to gauge it correctly. You arrive at this objective view, once you propose to a man that he change his name because of some event in his life. We do not even expect that he take his wife's name, for the notion of her civil inferiority is so deeply ingrained that this request would immediately smack of degradation and would cloud his judgment. No, he should assume another man's name, perhaps the name of his business partner within a professional association, and he is to use this name not only in all his professional transactions, but also in all personal matters. A Siegfried Schultz is to disappear, as if wiped off the blackboard with a wet sponge, and a new and shiny Siegfried Maier is to take his place. Would a man do that? I believe you would not find any man who would not revolt, even if his last name were Katzenbalg or Spanferkel.[1] So why does one impose this hurtful self-renunciation on women? There is in no sense any practical necessity, for both spouses can simply, as is customary in Switzerland, combine their names; the man could join his wife's name to his own and the wife do the same with his: Boos-Jegher, Schneeli-Beerli, Wirz-Baumann, etc. I already know the objection that will follow: but the children? This is as simple as it is feasible; depending on whether paternal or maternal rights take legal precedence, the children inherit the corresponding name of said parent, grow into it and perceive it to be an integral part of themselves. One grows fond of any name that one has been given at birth, as long as one is not forced to exchange it on command; that is an unbearable imposition.

I am fully convinced that your husband has no desire to wield his spousal authority; nevertheless, even after a period of 2 ½ years you are unable to foresee the development of your mutual relationship, for we are all human, and transience is the hallmark of all humanity. But

---

1   These names are meant to be humorous: *Katzenbalg* (literally "cat offspring" or "kitten") and *Spanferkel* (literally "roasted piglet").

even if both of you remained the same for the rest of your lives,——a companionship based on inequality, a marriage resting on a fundamental imbalance and subjugation between spouses, is not a companionship; it is not a marriage for sensitive human beings: a suggestion of shadow, a veil, thin as a cobweb, will always disrupt your mind's harmony, and this feeling will never fully leave you: my husband may grant me my full rights as an individual, but it is an act of mercy; in the eyes of the world I am a woman without any rights, that is, the woman who in Germany is the civilly married wife. And the world will ensure that on a daily basis you are made aware of your lack of rights; would you like a sampling of the needle pricks to expect? You wish to rent a studio for your work; the landlord asks you for your husband's written permission and wishes to sign the contract with him. The money courier delivers a cheque to your address; he hands it over to your husband, who is present, for him to sign and confirm that he has received the correct amount. You wish to withdraw a certain sum of money from the bank, where you deposit your income, and one has the impertinence to request your husband's signature before releasing it, even though it is your rightful income from your occupation, and thus reserved for your own use and discretion. You register your child at school, and here, too, one asks for the father's consent, etc. Let this selection, chosen from a plentiful history, suffice.

Will you wholly maintain your self-respect if you voluntarily place yourself in such a legal position? Will your marriage keep its dignity intact, when one of the spouses is elevated only through the other's consideration? And if you are willing to come to terms with these two arguments (although I hope not), are you also willing to accept the utter relinquishment of any right to your children, which German law imposes on the lawful mother? The German father is considered unrelated to his illegitimate child;——with this brutal sentence, German legislation establishes its conviction regarding natural father-child relationships; it implicitly admits the exclusive intimacy of the mother-child relationship. At the same time, the law states that the wife bears children for the husband, and only the husband; he exercises authority over their persons; he has the right to raise them, a right that, even in cases of strict abuse or fateful incompetence, is rarely restricted; he forfeits his parental rights only in the case of a criminal act directed against the child, not insofar as he has been found to have committed the crime, but only insofar as he has been sentenced to jail or prison time for more than six months. Furthermore, it is the father who determines the child's place of residence, its care and treatment; he dictates the principles of education; his consent alone is needed for the marriage of an underage daughter. If the mother is of the same opinion as he, she is allowed to participate in the decision-making; if her opinion differs, her objection is worthless, for "in the case of differences of opinion between parents, the father's opinion takes precedence."

Is not this formulation of parental rights, which exclusively favours the father, the crowning glory of a construction that reduces a lawful spouse to the spineless slave of her husband, since his power over the children, which will make the mother accede to anything, provides him with a ready hostage. And how are all those thousands of poor hostages disgracefully tortured by unscrupulous fathers——who, according to legal pronouncement, are themselves not related to their children, not even through the bonds of kinship and sympathy,—— seeking only to wound the mother through them. Can any self-respecting woman, in full knowledge of the legal situation, allow herself to be forced into such a degrading position in relation to her children, as is bound to happen if she enters into civil matrimony?

Enough,——I hope to have convinced you, if you sense your own strength and backbone, to be an individual and not a mere population statistic, that it is your duty to continue to tread that thorny path that you have already chosen. Better to suffer any kind of martyrdom than to relinquish yourself to civil marriage, for you are hereby building a bridge to the future. Believe me, once a hundred married couples, people of importance and value, have chosen to act as you, since for now only our very best are capable of acting in this way, then the gates to a possible moral marital union, sanctioned by law, will open, even for the average person. Once one-hundred capable German women have openly declared, our laws do not provide my husband and me with any possibility for maintaining human dignity within our relationship, then those laws will be changed. Do your part to initiate this reform.

Respectfully,
Irschenhausen, Upper Bavaria   Anita Augspurg

Appendix C: Anna Rüling on the Women's Movement and Homosexuality

1. Anna Rüling, "What Interest Does the Women's Movement Have in Solving the Homosexual Problem?," speech delivered at the Annual Meeting of the Scientific-Humanitarian Committee, Prinz Albrecht Hotel, Berlin, 8 October 1904

[Theodora Anna Sprüngli, or "Theo," went by the pseudonym Anna Rüling. Rüling (1880–1953), who was German, is known as the first lesbian activist. We are basing our translation on Rüling's original published text, "Welches Interesse hat die Frauenbewegung an der Lösung der homosexuellen Problems?," which appeared in *Jahrbuch für sexuelle Zwischenstufen unter besonderer Berücksichtigung der Homosexualität* [*Yearbook for Intermediate Sexual Types with Particular Consideration of Homosexuality*], vol. 7 (1905), pp. 130–51.]

Most honoured attendees!

The women's movement is a cultural-historical necessity!

Homosexuality is a necessity of natural history; it represents the connecting bridge, the natural, self-evident passage between man and woman. Today, this is an established scientific fact, against which ignorance and intolerance struggle in vain. Nevertheless, some may ask how I have arrived at naming both cultural-historical and scientific truths in the same breath, since, on the surface, they would seem to be two things diametrically opposed.

The reason for this widespread opinion is to be found in the general practice of only considering Uranian men when speaking of homosexuals[1] and overlooking how many homosexual women, although they

---

1 Urning and Uranian are terms popularized by Karl Heinrich Ulrichs (1825–95), Richard von Krafft-Ebing (1840–1902), John Addington Symonds (1840–93), Havelock Ellis (1859–1939), and Edward Carpenter (1844–1929). They refer to someone of the third sex, usually a person who, with a male body and a female psyche, is attracted to men, but also, on occasion, including at times in Rüling's speech, someone who, with a female body and a male psyche, is attracted to women. With regard to the latter kind of person, Rüling also uses the German terms *urnische Frau*, which we are translating as Uranian woman, and *Urnin* and *Urninde*, which we are translating as uraniad, a term that Xavier Mayne (Edward Prime-Stevenson [1858–1942]) employs in *The Intersexes: A History of Similisexualism as a Problem in Social Life* (1908). Rüling also uses *urning* as a generic term encompassing both male and female Uranians.

are rarely mentioned, there are, because——and I would almost say, unfortunately——they do not have to combat a criminal code that has arisen from unjust and false moral views.[1]

Women are not threatened by humiliating trials, or prison, when following their innate drive to love. But the emotional pressure that uraniads face is as heavy, even heavier, than the yoke under which their male counterparts suffer. To a world whose judgment is based on outward appearance, they are far more obvious than even the most effeminate Urning. All too often they are inundated with the mockery and scorn of moralistic ignorance.

Uranian women are, however, of at least as much importance to our entire social life as their male companions are, for, even though they are not spoken of, they influence our lives in manifold ways. When considering the facts, one soon arrives at the conclusion that homosexuality and the women's movement do not stand in opposition to each other, but instead that they are rather meant to aid each other in garnering rights[2] and respect, and in abolishing the injustice that condemns them.

The homosexual movement fights for the rights of all homosexuals, men as well as women. In contrast to all other movements that have, or should have, an interest in this struggle, the Scientific-Humanitarian Committee has distinguished itself through its lively dedication to uraniads.

The women's movement strives for the recognition of women's long-disregarded rights; in particular it fights for women's utmost independence and for women's legal equality with men, within matrimony and without. The latter endeavours are especially important, first because the economic conditions of our present time, and second because the statistically confirmed nominal surplus of women in our country's population have resulted in a large number of women who are unable to marry. Unless they come from independent means—— which is only the case for some 10%——these women are forced to do battle with life and earn their daily bread in some occupation or

---

1 Rüling is referring to Paragraph 175 of the German Criminal Code, which, between 1871 and 1994, criminalized sexual activity between men.

2 In the original German, the "each other in garnering rights" has a wider-than-normal spacing, which could indicate either a line justification issue or an emphasis on this particular moment in the speech. In this particular case, we attribute the spacing difference to line justification. We have footnoted subsequent textual moments in which spacing seems to indicate the same. In those instances in which larger spacing seems to indicate emphasis, we have italicized the relevant words and phrases.

another. Homosexual women's position toward and participation in one of the women's movement's most important concerns is of the greatest and most decisive significance and it merits the most widespread and extensive attention.

One must distinguish between two aspects of the homosexual woman: *her general personality and her sexual predisposition.*[1] The essential part, of course, is her general personality, the orientation of her sexual drive is only secondary; without an exact knowledge and acknowledgement of the latter, one will never be able to judge her fully and justly, for the physical drive to love is almost always only an outflow, a natural consequence of psychological qualities; i.e., in people with predominantly male characteristics it will, according to nature, direct itself towards women and vice versa, without nature always taking into consideration the external physical build of the person. The homosexual woman possesses many qualities, tendencies and abilities commonly considered the legally valid attributes of a man. In particular, the track of her emotional life does not follow the standard female route. Whereas with the decidedly heterosexual woman feeling is almost always predominant and decisive——also here exceptions prove the rule——with the uraniad it is clear-eyed reason that generally prevails. Like the average, normal man, she is more objective, energetic, and goal-oriented than the feminine woman, her thoughts and feelings are those of a man; *she does not imitate him but is of his predisposition, this is the crucial, determining point*[2] that those who hate and denounce the "man-woman" always disregard, because they never once take the trouble thoroughly to study the homosexual phenomenon. It is so easy to judge what one does not understand, as easy as it is seemingly difficult to revise a preconceived and faulty notion, or to let enlightenment correct it. I wish to remark at this point that there exist an absolute and a merely psychological homosexuality, so that masculine characteristics do not necessarily result in a sexual drive toward one's own sex; for each uraniad also naturally possesses feminine qualities, either more or less numerous, which, considering the vastly differing gradations in the transition between the sexes, may also well express themselves in a sexual drive toward a man. Of course, in most of these cases, this drive seeks to exert itself toward a very feminine man, as the natural complement to a woman with a strongly masculine soul. As proof of this claim I need only remind you of George Sand and Daniel Stern, both of whom loved men who were among the most effeminate men of all time,

---

1 Emphasis in original.
2 Emphasis in original.

Friedrich Chopin and Franz Liszt.[1] The great artist Klara Schumann, too, was married to a man with strong feminine tendencies——Robert Schumann.[2] It appears, by the way, as if the sexual drive was never developed very strongly in those women whom I have labelled psychologically homosexual; George Sand and Daniel Stern, too, loved their artists far more with their souls than with their senses. I am therefore inclined in the case of psychologically homogenic[3] women to speak as it were of "unsexual" natures. Since a homosexual woman, with her masculine tendencies and attributes, can never be the fitting *complement*[4] of the man who is all man, it is undoubtedly clear that the uraniad is not suited for marriage. Uranian women themselves are usually well aware of as much, or at least feel it subconsciously, and, according to their nature, resist the march to the registry office. But how often have they not counted on parents, cousins, aunts and all their dear friends and relations, who, telling them, day in, day out, of the necessity of marriage, make the women's lives miserable with their sage advice. Often, they stumble blindly into a marriage, thanks to the girls' imprudent education, which leaves them without any clear view and understanding of sexuality and sexual life. As long as so-called "society" maintains the view that old-maidhood, that is, a woman's unmarried state, is something unpleasant, even inferior, the uraniad will all too often allow external circumstances to drive her into a marriage, *in which she can neither find nor create happiness.*[5] Certainly, such a marriage is far more immoral than a love relationship between two human beings drawn mightily to each other by a powerful force.

The women's movement wishes to reform marriage.——It wants to make many legal changes, so that today's often unappealing conditions shall end; so that discontent and lawlessness, despotism and slavish submission shall disappear from the family home; so that a healthier and stronger generation shall flourish.

In these reformist efforts, the women's movement must not forget the extent to which the false assessment of homosexual women has led

---

1 Born Amantine Lucile Aurore Dupin (1804–76), George Sand was a French writer. Marie Cathérine Sophie de Flavigny (1805–76), another French writer, wrote under the pseudonym "Daniel Stern." Frédéric Chopin (1810–49) was a Polish composer and pianist, and Franz Liszt (1811–86) a Hungarian composer and pianist.

2 Klara Schumann (1819–96) and her husband, Robert Schumann (1810–56), were German composers and pianists.

3 For an early use of the term "homogenic" referring to homosexual love, see Carpenter.

4 Emphasis in original.

5 Emphasis in original.

to unfavourable circumstances; I intentionally say "the extent to which"; of course, I do not wish to attribute all the blame to this false assessment. But even for this partial blame alone, it is the women's movement's plain and undeniable duty to clarify for the broad masses, through both the spoken and the written word, how detrimental marriage is for homosexuals. First and foremost, of course, for the two parties involved. The man is simply being cheated, since apart from its idealistic meaning, marriage is a mutual contract in which both parties assume rights and responsibilities. A homosexual woman, however, can only fulfil her duties toward the man with disdain, at best with indifference. A forced sexual union is undoubtedly torturous for the two people involved, and no decent, thoughtful man can view it as something desirable, nor can he find with a Uranian woman the happiness that he sought in marriage. It happens very often that such a man, out of a sense of decency toward the woman, avoids sexual intercourse with her, and then seeks to satisfy his urge in the arms of a mistress or with prostitutes. But anyone who honestly values the true morality and health of our people, as the women's movement does, must do all that he can to prevent homosexuals from marrying. And the women's movement can do ever so much to enlighten people, so that all circles recognise that the marriage of uraniads is a three-fold injustice, against the state, against society, and against an unborn generation, for experience teaches us that the progeny of Uranians is only in the rarest of cases healthy and strong. The unhappy creatures, conceived without love, even without desire, constitute a large percentage of the feebleminded, idiots, epileptics, consumptives, *degenerates*[1] of all sorts. Diseased sexual urges, like sadism and masochism, too, are often the legacy of Uranians who, against their own nature, begat children. The state and society have a pressing interest in Uranians not marrying, for they will later bear not the least part of the burden of caring for such sick and feeble creatures, from whom they can hardly expect anything in return.

It seems to me that one essential practical point for heterosexual women is this:[2] if uraniads could remain unmarried without damaging their social status, heterosexual women would in turn, according to their own natural predisposition, more readily find a generally satisfying role as wife, homemaker, and mother. We still unfortunately lack exact statistics regarding the number of homosexual women; however, given my vast experience and intense study in this area, we are able to

---

1 Emphasis in original. Rüling's degeneracy argument here reflects the eugenic thinking that was widespread among sexologists and members of the women's movement.

2 Emphasis in original.

assume that the results of Dr. Hirschfeld's statistical surveys on the prevalence of male homosexuality can also be applied to women. Hence, there would be approximately the same number of Uranians as single women in Germany. This must not be misunderstood. For example, I wish to state that there are two million single women and two million homosexual women. Among these two million single women, there is already naturally a larger percentage who are Uranians, let us say 50 %, or one million; but among homosexual women, in turn, there are about 50% who, due to external circumstances, have married, and as you will certainly figure out, have thus blocked the 50% of normal, single women from marrying. It is easy enough to draw a conclusion. Were all uraniads to remain unmarried, the likelihood of marriage for heterosexual women would rise significantly, though I do not wish to imply that a universal remedy for old-maidhood has herewith been found, since men's increasing animosity toward marriage is in many cases rooted in social conditions that are best addressed in another context.

Were it to focus on the homosexual aspect of the marriage question, the women's movement would also then take a further step on the path toward the beautiful and noble goal of doing justice to the original idea of marriage, the loving union between man and woman. For it is an ethical imperative, today so often affronted by marriages of convenience and those made for pecuniary gain, that people should only enter the bonds of matrimony out of love.

I have noticed that many homosexual women marry because they realise their nature too late, and thus, through no fault of their own, they suffer from and they create unhappiness. Here, too, the women's movement can intervene with a helping hand, in that, when addressing questions concerning the education of young people——as frequently occurs——it lays out the necessity of enlightening older children and adolescents, in whom parents have, after long, loving and careful observation, noticed a homosexual drive——and honest and discerning observers can recognise as much from numerous signs—— clarifying for them the nature of homosexuality and their own nature in a sensible and comprehensible manner. In this way, they could prevent endless early suffering and much misery, instead of——as often happens——using all of their means to attempt to force homosexual children into heterosexual pathways. One need not thereby fear that sensitive heterosexual children might by chance be regarded as homosexual and thus be fashioned into homosexuals, because, first, such an explanation would only occur after a consultation with a physician experienced in this area, and, second, experience has already shown us that neither seduction nor anything else can change a heterosexual drive into a homosexual one or vice versa. Certainly, a heterosexual person can allow himself to be seduced into homosexual activities, but this happens out of curiosity, a craving for pleasure, or as a surrogate for normal intercourse that is lacking——the latter can, for example, sometimes be seen among sailors——the innate sexual drive, however, is not thereby altered and, under normal circumstances, will always dominate the field.

At this point, I myself would like to state once again what Dr. Hirschfeld has already explained numerous times, namely that homosexuality is not an occurrence attending one particular social class; that it does not occur more frequently in the higher classes than the lower ones or vice versa. No father or mother, and so not any one of you, honoured attendees who have children, can be certain from the outset whether among his offspring there is not a Uranian child. Oddly enough, in middle-class circles, it is assumed that there is no place for homosexuality, and it is from these circles as well that the most ardent enemies of the movement for the liberation of Uranians are recruited. *As an example of this assertion, I would like to mention my father, who, when the conversation once accidentally turned to the topic of homosexuality, explained with confident conviction: "This kind of thing could never happen in my family!" The facts prove the opposite!*[1] I don't think I need to add anything further!

Returning to the marriage question, I would like to remark that a homosexual woman almost never becomes a so-called "old maid." This is a remarkable circumstance, because it renders uraniads easily recognisable, especially in their old age. Consider for a moment an unmarried homosexual woman between the ages of 30 and 50; in her you will find none of the so often ridiculed characteristics of unmarried heterosexual women. This observation is instructive, because it proves that a reasonable and measured satisfaction of the sexual drive also keeps women cheerful, lively, and capable, while absolute sexual abstinence easily develops and enhances the very characteristics we perceive as unpleasant in the old maid: e.g., unkindness, hysterical irritability, etc.

But now, in order to create the opportunity for homosexuals, and for all women in general, to live according to their natures, it is absolutely necessary to actively join the women's movement in its efforts to open up more educational possibilities and new professions for women. I will first touch upon the age-old point of contention regarding the value of the sexes. I believe that, with a bit of good will, one could easily find agreement, if here again one considers infallible nature's intentions in creating man, woman, and the transitions between the two. And then one must needs arrive at the conclusion

---

1 Emphasis in original.

that it is wrong to deem one sex superior to the other——to speak of a first-class sex,——man——a second-class——woman——and a third-class——the Uranian.

The sexes are not different *in value*; they are merely different *in kind*.[1] The women's movement can do nothing to alter this fact, from which it naturally and clearly follows that men, women and urnings are *not equally suited for all occupations*[2]—nor would its sensible faction want as much. The feminine woman is already, by virtue of nature, organically determined first and foremost to be a wife and mother. And she has every right to be proud of this, her natural destiny, for there is no occupation to be valued more highly than that of mother! The woman who is wife and mother, or one of the two, needs of course not forget the entire rest of the world——she should rather partake in her well-measured share of all events of public life——that she may be able to do so is the goal of the woman's movement, and this is most assuredly one of its most beautiful goals.

Nature has assigned the normal, that is, the thoroughly masculine man, many other functions, and indicated different paths for him than for a woman. He is—undeniably—most often already physically more predestined for an arduous life struggle than is a woman; so that there are occupations open to him, which are automatically fore-closed for her, e.g., the profession of soldier, all professions demand-ing hard physical labour, etc. Of course, here, too, there is a bridge on which we find those occupations that men and women can perform equally well, depending on their particular individualities. The logic of the opponents of the women's movement suffers mainly from the fact that it has gathered all women together under the collective term "woman" without considering that nature has created no two beings entirely alike. When judging a person's suitability for a profession, his inner personality is the one and only thing that matters, which again is a result of that mixture of his masculine and feminine attributes. We can therefore differentiate among an individuality that is female, in which feminine qualities prevail, an individuality that is male, in which masculine qualities prevail, and finally a male-female or female-male individuality, in which an approximately equal mixture of both is present.

When nature created the sexes differently, it most certainly did not wish to say that there could only be one sphere of activity for a woman——the home——and a different one for a man——the

---

1 Emphases in original.

2 Here, Rüling uses the term *urning* as a general term for both male and female Uranians. Emphasis in original.

world.——Instead, nature's intention was and undoubtedly is for every human being to have the opportunity to obtain the position that, according to his qualities and abilities, he is able to fulfill.

The component ratio of masculine and feminine qualities is so infinitely variable among human beings that it is a matter of simple justice to raise each child——regardless of whether male or female—to be *independent. Once grown, they will then need to decide for themselves whether their nature propels them into the home or the world, into marriage or unmarried life.*[1] There must be a free play of energy; that is the best and safest way to distinguish between women who can and want to take up a profession, whether artistic or academic, outside the home, and women who do not find the strength within themselves to do so. And again, it is the parents who should see it as their sacred duty to do justice to each child's individuality and under all circumstances to avoid a formulaic approach to raising them. It is of course a different matter with schools, which cannot do without a certain formulaic approach, which needs, however, in the future to be consistent among boys and girls, so that the old delusion that girls' brains are less capable of learning than boys' brains can be eliminated.

There is no need to fear that equal education and educational opportunities for girls and boys will result in immeasurable competition across the professions——especially, as hostile parties claim, in the academic professions. Homosexual women are especially suited for these scholarly professions, since they possess the very qualities of greater objectivity, capability, and stamina that feminine women most often lack. This observation does not of course preclude that among our female doctors, lawyers, etc. there are also highly capable heterosexual women. I would, however, still argue that the vast majority of heterogenic[2] women will, under favourable conditions, almost always and in any case much rather seek happiness in marriage. Such a woman will therefore principally strive for a more profound and well-rounded education for the female sex in order that she might be a companion equal to the husband, one whom he loves not only with his senses, but one whom he respects because he recognises that she stands on his same intellectual level, and to whom he will then unquestionably grant the same rights that he possesses.

Men, women, and homosexuals thus benefit equally from a more purposeful education, as well as from the broadest educational opportunities for male and female youth. The men gain rational and under-

---

1 Emphasis in original.
2 Heterogenic here means heterosexual. Ellis uses this term in *Sexual Inversion*, 3rd ed.

standing life partners; the women gradually gain a more dignified and legally more respected position; and uraniads can freely devote themselves to professions of their liking.

Much as the homosexual man often prefers occupations that tend toward the feminine, such as dressmaking, nursing, or the position of cook or servant, there are also professions for which Uranian women are especially suited; as experience teaches us, there are particularly large numbers of homosexual women in the medical, legal, agricultural, and free-lance artistic professions.

There are men who, like Weininger,[1] claim that all the notable, significant, or famous women in the fields of history, literature, science or anything else were homosexual. Following my previous explanations, I probably do not especially need to emphasise that I consider this very one-sided view unproven, since not only history, but also our own observations daily teach us the untenability of this theory. Alternatively, it can and should not be denied that many significant women were indeed homosexually inclined——I shall only mention Sappho, Christine of Sweden, Sonja Kowalewska, Rosa Bonheur.[2] In contrast, it would certainly seem quite strange to count Elizabeth of England[3] and Catherine the Great of Russia[4] among the Uranians; the latter might possibly have been bisexual——her many male and female "friendships" at least suggest as much——in any case she was not purely homosexual.

In contrast to the anti-feminists, who declare the female sex to be inferior and who wish only to validate women who exhibit strong masculine characteristics, I consider women in themselves to be equal to men, yet I am convinced that the homosexual woman is especially

---

1   Otto Weininger (1880–1903) was the author of *Geschlecht und Charakter* [*Sex and Character*]. The name is here more widely spaced than the rest of the sentence.

2   Sappho (c. 630–c. 570 BCE), an ancient Greek from the island of Lesbos, is one of the greatest of lyric poets and a major figure in lesbian literature, from whose name and birthplace the words "sapphic" and "lesbian" derive; Queen Christina (1626–89) ruled Sweden from 1632 to 1654; Sofia Kovalevskaya (1850–91), also known as Sonia Kovalevsky, was a Russian mathematician; Rosa Bonheur (1822–99) was a French painter.

3   Queen Elizabeth I of England (1533–1603), the last of the Tudor monarchs, ruled for over 44 years (1558–1603) and oversaw a period of both relative political stability and literary flowering.

4   Catherine the Great (1729–96), Russia's longest ruling female monarch (r. 1762–96), proved one of its most effective, expanding both its territory and its influence.

suited to play a leading role in the larger women's rights movement encompassing all civilised nations.

And indeed——from the very first days of the women's movement until today——it has been, in no small part, homogenic women who, in the numerous battles, have assumed leadership; who primarily with their energy have made the naturally indifferent and readily submissive average woman aware of her human dignity and her innate rights.

I can and will not name any names, for as long as homosexuality is still in many circles regarded as something criminal and contrary to nature, as something diseased at best, ladies whom I would describe as homosexual may feel offended. In general, decency and duty forbid indiscretion, and the noble feelings of love belonging to a Uranian women's rights advocate have no more place in a public forum than do any sentiments belonging to heterosexuals. Whosoever has even superficially followed the development of the women's movement, whosoever has met or recognised some or many of the movement's leading women, and even if only possessing the slightest bit of understanding regarding the signs of homosexuality, will soon discern the uraniads among the women's rights advocates and will recognise that they are not among the most ineffectual.

If we consider all the contributions that homosexual women for decades have made to the women's movement, it is astonishing that to this day the large and influential organisations of this movement have failed to lift a finger to help their not insignificant number of Uranian members, to acquire their civil and social rights. It is astonishing that these organisations have done nothing, *absolutely nothing at all*,[1] to enlighten the general public about the true nature of Uranism and in so doing to protect some of their best-known and most deserving pioneers from mockery and derision. It would not even be that difficult to point out how homosexual tendencies often manifest themselves involuntarily, in appearance, language, posture, movement, dress, etc., without the slightest deliberate effort on the person's part; and how uraniads are wholly unjustly exposed to the heartless ridicule of rough or ignorant people. Yet it should also be noted that, naturally, homosexual women do not always display a masculine outward appearance that is in harmony with their nature. There are also numerous uraniads who have entirely feminine exteriors, which they themselves, out of fear of having their homosexuality become known, emphasise through feminine behaviour, a farce that, of course, often enrages them, and one under which they suffer greatly.

---

1 Emphasis in original.

I know very well the reason for this complete and doubly noticeable restraint within the women's movement——which otherwise even treats purely sexual matters with rare frankness and matter-of-factness. There is the fear that by broaching the homosexual question, by energetically advocating for Uranians' human rights, the movement might harm itself in the eyes of the still blind and ignorant masses. I gladly concede that this fear was justified in the infancy of the movement, when it had carefully to avoid losing its newly won allies. That was a thoroughly unobjectionable excuse for temporarily and completely ignoring the homosexual question

Today, however, when the movement is unstoppable in its progress, when no bureaucratic wisdom, no philistinism can any longer impede the movement's triumphant march; today I say that the complete disregard of a question that is undoubtedly very important is an injustice, an injustice that, in large part, the women's movement is perpetrating against itself. The so-called "moderate" faction will certainly never set to work on behalf of homosexuals, for the simple reason that this faction is not prone to any action at all. One day, victory will be gained under the banner of radicalism, and it is those radicals whom we expect to finally break the spell and honestly and openly admit: yes, there are among us a large number of uraniads who have afforded us a full supply of effort and work and many a beautiful victory. It's not as if I would want to see all the questions of the women's movement treated from the viewpoint of homosexuality; as if I would want to credit uraniads with all or even most of the achievements;——that would probably be as foolish as it is wrong not to consider the homosexual question at all.

No doubt the women's movement has larger and more important tasks to fulfil than the liberation of homosexuals,——but it can only do justice to large tasks if it does not carelessly leave smaller tasks aside.

The women's movement should not therefore elevate the homosexual question to particular prominence. The movement need not preach in the markets and streets of the unfair critique of Uranians. ——It would not be able to do so without actually harming itself—— I am not denying this side of the issue at all. It only has to accord the homosexual question its rightful place, when discussing the sexual, ethical, economic, and purely humane relationships of the sexes to each other. This the movement can do, and in so doing it can also, slowly and without much ado, effect enlightenment.

I now come to an issue with which the women's movement has been especially preoccupied over the last few years,——I am speaking of prostitution. From an ethical standpoint, one can think what one will, but in any case, given the circumstances, we will continue to have to reckon with it for a long time to come. Personally, I consider prostitution an unfortunate but necessary evil that will be impossible to eliminate as long as human passions exist; but one that, at best, we will be able to keep somewhat in check,——a goal that, after all, is worth the effort.

That evidently some 20% of prostitutes are homosexual seems to me of not insignificant and of, until now, entirely overlooked importance for the women's movement's struggle against prostitution's prevalence, and therefore against nation-destroying venereal diseases. This may, at first seem strange, since homosexuality and regular sexual intercourse with men are seemingly so contradictory. In response to my question of how a uraniad could become a prostitute, more than one "street girl" answered that she understood her sad trade to be purely business,——her sexual drive was not a concern, for it was satisfied by her female beloved. Adverse domestic and economic conditions had driven these girls into the street.

If the women's movement were able to open all suitable professions to women, to implement a fair evaluation of an individual's characteristics and predisposition, then there would soon be no more homosexual harlot, and a great many heterosexual girls who, fleeing bad social circumstances, run into the arms of prostitution today would also be able to provide for themselves in a better and more dignified way. From the outset they would endeavour to find an occupation, because in their youth they would have been raised more sensibly so as to be independent. A girl who early on has been steeled to face life's struggles is far less likely to end up on the street than a girl who thoughtlessly and carelessly lives her life without any knowledge of the simplest and most natural things. In some sense, the homogenic woman's battle for social recognition is also a battle against prostitution, whereby I need emphasise again that this battle can only ever be about restriction, not full suppression.

It should not be forgotten that were uranism on the whole to be judged in a fair manner, a large number of homosexual men, who today frequent prostitutes against their own nature, out of fear that their predisposition could be made public, would cease to do so. This, in turn, would naturally result in a decrease in venereal diseases, which, though of course not sizable, would still in my view be of value, since every single case in which a syphilitic or other venereal infection is avoided signifies a gain for the health of our people and therefore for the coming generation, upon whom the good and greatness of our fatherland rests.——

The women's movement is fighting for the right to a free personality and to self-determination. It has to admit to itself that the curse that society continues to hurl at Uranians, suppresses that very right, and therefore it is the movement's duty to stand with homosexuals in this struggle, just as it stands with unwed mothers, working-class women, and many others whom it energetically and helpfully supports in their struggle for freedom and justice, in their struggle against old, wrongful beliefs concerning a decency that is in actuality an indecency, a morality that, in the light of day, reveals itself to be an immorality of the worst kind. Much as women possess an age-old human right that, at one time taken from them by brute force, they now want bravely to reclaim, so, too, Uranians have an innate, age-old natural right to their love, which is noble and pure, like heterosexual love when experienced by good human beings. Good human beings exist among homosexuals, much as they do among the so-called "normal."

Most of all I wish to avoid creating the impression that I am over-estimating Uranians. I can assure you, honoured attendees, I am not; ——I know the faults and weaknesses of homosexuals all too well, but I also know their good sides, and therefore I may say: Uranians are never, ever better, but they are also not any worse as human beings than heterosexuals are,——they are not different in value, just different in kind.

In summary, I wish to emphasise once more that the Uranian woman has in every way played her good part in all of the questions that concern our women's movement at large; she has often been the one who has taken a single action and set things into motion; because of her characteristics, which incline toward the masculine, she naturally perceives doubly the many, many injustices and hardships that laws, society and outdated morality impose on women;——without the capable participation of uraniads, today's women's movement would not have come as far as it in fact has,——which could be easily proven with examples.

The women's movement and the movement for homosexual rights have long trod a gloomy path, and in their way encountered countless obstacles. Now, slowly, it is brightening, brightening around us and within the human heart. Not that the difficult struggle for the rights of women and Uranians is already over; in both cases we still stand in the midst of combat and many a heated battle will still need to be won; many a victim of wrongful judgment, of unfortunate and misguided law will still have to fall, exhausted and mortally wounded, before both movements achieve their goal——personality's freedom. The summit will be reached much before that, however, when both movements recognise that they share many a common interest, if they peacefully join hands to fight together where necessary.

And if earnest and difficult times are still to meet them both, that does not mean that one should lose heart like a coward; instead, one must bravely burst through enemy lines, on to certain victory. For the light of knowledge and truth has risen in the east,——no force of gloom can still hold back the bright course of the sun,——which will slowly rise higher and higher! Neither today nor tomorrow but in a not too distant future, the women's movement and Uranians will plant their flags and claim victory!

Per aspera ad astra![1]

---

1 Latin: through difficulties to the stars.

Appendix D: Havelock Ellis and Female Inversion

1. From Havelock Ellis and John Addington Symonds, "Sexual Inversion in Women," *Sexual Inversion* (Wilson and Macmillan, 1897), pp. 77–103

[A major English sexologist and an early researcher on transgenderism, Havelock Ellis (1859–1939) was also a supporter of eugenics. *Sexual Inversion* eventually became part of his multi-volume *Studies in the Psychology of Sex* (1933). John Addington Symonds (1840–93) was an English poet, literary critic, and scholar. His *A Problem in Greek Ethics* (1883), included in *Sexual Inversion*, provides a key discussion of Greek male love.]

Homosexuality has been observed in women from very early times, and in very widespread regions. Refraining from any attempt to trace its history, and coming down to Europe in the seventeenth century, we find a case of sexual inversion in a woman, which seems to be recorded in greater detail than any case in a man had yet been recorded ...[1] Moreover, Westphal's first notable case, which may be said to inaugurate the scientific study of sexual inversion, was in a woman.[2] This passage of women from women has, also, formed a favourite subject with the novelist, who has until lately been careful to avoid the same subject as presented in the male. It seems probable that homosexuality is little, if at all, less common than in man.[3]

Yet we know comparatively little of sexual inversion in woman; of the total number of recorded cases of this abnormality, now very considerable, but a small proportion are in women, and the chief monographs on the subject devote but little space to women.

I think there are several reasons for this. Notwithstanding the severity with which homosexuality in women has been visited in a few

---

1 With the exception of note 3 below, we have not included any of the footnotes that are in the original text. We have also omitted various sections of the main text, including ones that discuss women's inversion in relation to racial hierarchy.

2 Karl Friedrich Otto Westphal (1833–90). His 1870 paper on "contrary sexual feeling" was a key contribution to sexological studies.

3 [Excerpt from original footnote:] As regards Germany, see Moll, *Die Conträre Sexualempfindung*, 2nd ed., p. 315. It is noteworthy that a considerable proportion of the number of cases in which inversion has led to crimes of violence, or otherwise acquired medico-legal importance, has been among women.

cases, for the most part men seem to have been indifferent towards it; when it has been made a crime or a cause for divorce in men, it has usually been considered as no offence at all in women ... Another reason is that it is less easy to detect in women; we are accustomed to a much greater familiarity and intimacy between women than between men, and we are less apt to suspect the existence of any abnormal passion. And allied with this cause we have also to bear in mind the extreme ignorance and the extreme reticence of women regarding any abnormal or even normal manifestation of their sexual life. A woman may feel a high degree of sexual attraction for another woman without realising that her affection is sexual, and when she does realise it she is nearly always very unwilling to reveal the nature of her intimate experience, even with the adoption of precautions, and although the fact may be present to her that by helping to reveal the nature of her abnormality she may be helping to lighten the burden of it on other women. Among the numerous confessions voluntarily sent to Krafft-Ebing there is not one by a woman. There is, I think, one other reason why sexual inversion is less obvious in a woman. We have some reason to believe that, while a slight degree of homosexuality is commoner in women than in men, and is favoured by the conditions under which women live, well marked and fully developed cases of inversion are rarer in women than in men. This result would be in harmony with what we know as to the greater affectability of the feminine organism to slight stimuli, and its less liability to serious variation....

The same kind of aberrations that are found among men in lower races are also seen in women, though they are less frequently recorded ...

In theatres this cause [for the development of homosexuality] is associated with the general tendency for homosexuality to be connected with dramatic aptitude, a point to which I shall have to refer later on. I am indebted to a friend for the following note: "Passionate friendships among girls, from the most innocent to the most elaborate excursions in the direction of Lesbos,[1] are extremely common in theatres, both among actresses and, even more, among chorus and ballet girls. Here the pell-mell of the dressing-rooms, the wait of perhaps two hours between the performances, during which all the girls are cooped up, in a state of inaction and excitement, in a few crowded dressing-rooms, affords every opportunity for the growth of this particular kind of sentiment. In most of the theatres there is a little circle of girls, somewhat avoided by the others, or themselves careless of further acquaintanceship, who profess the most unbounded devotion to one another. Most of these girls are equally ready to flirt with the opposite

1 Here, "the direction of Lesbos" refers to lesbianism.

sex, but I know certain ones among them who will scarcely speak to a man, and who are never seen without their particular 'pal' or 'chum,' who, if she gets moved to another theatre, will come round and wait for her friend at the stage-door. But here again it is but seldom that the experience is carried very far. The fact is that the English girl, especially of the lower and middle classes, whether she has lost her virtue or not, is extremely fettered by conventional notions. Ignorance and habit are two restraining influences from the carrying out of this particular kind of perversion to its logical conclusions. It is, therefore, among the upper ranks, alike of society and of prostitution, that Lesbianism is most definitely to be met with, for here we have much greater liberty of action, and much greater freedom from prejudices."

... A class of women to be first mentioned, a class in which homosexuality, while fairly distinct, is only slightly marked, is formed by the women to whom the actively inverted woman is most attracted. These women differ in the first place from the normal or average woman in that they are not repelled or disgusted by lover-like advances from persons of their own sex. They are not usually attractive to the average man, though to this rule there are many exceptions. Their faces may be plain or ill-made, but not seldom they possess good figures, a point which is apt to carry more weight with the inverted woman than beauty of face. Their sexual impulses are seldom well marked, but they are of strongly affectionate nature. On the whole, they are women who are not very robust and well-developed, physically or nervously, and who are not well adopted for child-bearing, but who still possess many excellent qualities, and they are always womanly. One may perhaps say that they are the pick of the women whom the average man would pass by. No doubt this is often the reason why they are open to homosexual advances, but I do not think it is the sole reason. So far as they may be said to constitute a class, they seem to possess a genuine though not precisely sexual preference for women over men, and it is this coldness rather than lack of charm which often renders men rather indifferent to them.

The actively inverted woman differs from the woman of the class just mentioned in one fairly essential character: a more or less distinct trace of masculinity. She may not be, and frequently is not, what would be called a "mannish" woman, for the latter may imitate men on grounds of taste and habit unconnected with sexual perversion, while in the inverted woman the masculine traits are part of an organic instinct which she by no means always wishes to accentuate. The inverted woman's masculine element may in the least degree consist only in the fact that she makes advances to the woman to whom she is attracted and treats all men in a cool, direct manner, which may not exclude comradeship, but which excludes every sexual relationship, whether of passion or merely of coquetry. As a rule the inverted woman feels absolute indifference towards men, and not seldom repulsion. And this feeling, as a rule, is instinctively reciprocated by men....

... [I]t is, indeed, noteworthy that women seem with special frequency to fall in love with disguised persons of their own sex ... There is, however, a very pronounced tendency among sexually inverted women to adopt male attire when practicable. In such cases male garments are not usually regarded as desirable chiefly on account of practical convenience, nor even in order to make an impression on other women, but because the wearer feels more at home in them ... And when they still retain female garments these usually show some traits of masculine simplicity, and there is nearly always a disdain for the petty feminine artifices of the toilet. Even when this is not obvious there are all sorts of instinctive gestures and habits which may suggest to female acquaintances the remark that such a person "ought to have been a man." The brusque, energetic movements, the attitude of the arms, the direct speech, the inflexions of the voice, the masculine straightforwardness and sense of honour, and especially the attitude towards men, free from any suggestion either of shyness or audacity, will often suggest the underlying psychic abnormality to a keen observer ... Although there is sometimes a certain general coarseness of physical texture, we do not find any trace of a beard or moustache ...

The inverted woman is an enthusiastic admirer of feminine beauty, especially of the statuesque beauty of the body, unlike in this the normal woman whose sexual emotion is but faintly tinged by aesthetic feeling. In her sexual habits we rarely find the degree of promiscuity which is not uncommon among inverted men ...

It has been stated by many observers who are able to speak with some authority—in America, in France, in Germany, in England— that homosexuality is increasing among women ... It seems probable that this is true. There are many influences in our civilisation to-day which encourage such manifestations. The modern movement of emancipation—the movement to obtain the same rights and duties, the same freedom and responsibility, the same education and the same work—must be regarded as, on the whole, a wholesome and inevitable movement. But it carries with it certain disadvantages. It has involved an increase in feminine criminality and in feminine insanity, which are being elevated towards the masculine standard. In connection with these we can scarcely be surprised to find an increase in homosexuality which has always been regarded as belonging to an allied, if not the same, group of phenomena. Woman [sic] are, very justly, coming to look upon knowledge and experience generally as their right as much as their brothers' right. But when this doctrine is applied to the sexual sphere it finds certain limitations. Intimacies of any kind between young men and young woman [sic] are as much discouraged socially now as ever they were; as regards higher education, the mere association of the sexes in the lecture-room or the laboratory or the hospital is discouraged in England and in America. Marriage is decaying, and while men are allowed freedom, the sexual field of women is becoming restricted to trivial flirtation with the opposite sex, and to intimacy with their own sex; having been taught independence of men and disdain for the old theory which placed women in the moated grange of the home to sigh for a man who never comes, a tendency develops for women to carry this independence still further and to find love where they find work. I do not say that these unquestionable influences of modern movements can directly cause sexual inversion, though they may indirectly, in so far as they promote hereditary neurosis; but they develop the germs of it, and they probably cause a spurious imitation. This spurious imitation is due to the fact that the congenital anomaly occurs with special frequency in woman [sic] of high intelligence who, voluntarily or involuntarily, influence others ...

Appendix E: Cover Images from Draisena

1. Cover of 24 April 1899 edition of *Draisena*

2. Closeup of cover image from 26 October 1898

[Image of Mlle. J Beau, Paris. *Draisena*, vol. 4, no. 34 (26 October 1898), p. 547. Courtesy of the Österreichische Nationalbibliothek, Vienna. Image 452.353-D]

Mlle. Pauline, Paris.
Originalaufnahme von J. Beau, Paris.

Appendix F: Cover Image from Adelt-Duc's Novella Collection

1. Cover image of *Indische Novellen* (1914)

Works Cited and Select Bibliography

Works by Mina Adelt-Duc

Adelt-Duc, Mina. *Des Hauses Tausendkünstler. Ein treuer Rathgeber für den Haushalt.* A. Michow, 1891.

——. *Des Pastors Liebe. Ein modernes Sittenbild.* Cäsar Schmidt, 1904.

——. *Die Emmaus-Frage. Auch eine Kritik der reinen Vernunft.* Herrcke und Lebeling, 1905.

——, editor. *Draisena. Blätter für Damenradfahren. Organ zur Pflege und Förderung des Radfahrens der Damen.* Dresden and Vienna, 1895–99.

——. *3½ Monate Fabrik-Arbeiterin.* J. Leiser, 1893.

——. *Ich will! Freier Wille der Frau und die Folge des Durchsetzens des Willens gegen allen gesellschaftlichen Zwang.* Richard Eckstein Nachfolger, 1902.

——. *Indische Novellen.* G. Müller-Mann'sche Verlagsbuchhandlung, 1914.

——. *Macht euch frei! Ein Wort an die deutschen Frauen.* Deutsche Schriftsteller-Genossenschaft, 1893.

——. *Sind es Frauen? Roman über das dritte Geschlecht.* Richard Eckstein Nachfolger, 1901.

——. *Südindien und Burma.* H.J. Koeppen, 1909.

On Lesbians, the Third Sex, and German Women's Rights Movement at the Turn of the Century—Primary Texts

Anonymous [Emilie Knopf]. *Der Liebe Lust und Leid der Frau zur Frau.* Verlagsbureau für literarische Neuheiten, 1895.

Anonymous. *Noli me tangere! Dunkle Punkte aus dem modernen Frauenleben.* Max Spohr Verlag, 1897.

Augspurg, Anita. "Ein typischer Fall der Gegenwart. Ein offener Brief." *Die Frauenbewegung: Revue für die Interessen der Frauen*, vol. 11, no. 11, 1905, pp. 81–82.

——. "Ein typischer Fall der Gegenwart. Ein offener Brief." *Europa. Wochenschrift für Kultur und Politik*, vol. 1, no. 7, 1905, pp. 311–14.

Carpenter, Edward. *Homogenic Love and Its Place in a Free Society.* The Labour Press Society, 1894.

Dauthendey, Elisabeth. "Die Urnische Frage und die Frau." *Jahrbuch für sexuelle Zwischenstufen*, vol. 8, 1906, pp. 285–300.

——. *Vom neuen Weibe und seiner Liebe. Ein Buch für reife Geister.* Schuster & Loeffler, 1901.

Elberskirchen, Johanna. *Die Liebe des dritten Geschlechts. Homosexualität, eine bisexuelle Varietät—keine Entartung, keine Schuld.* Max Spohr, 1904.

——. *Was hat der Mann aus Weib, Kind und sich gemacht? Revolution und Erlösung des Weibes. Eine Abrechnung mit dem Mann—Ein Wegweiser in die Zukunft!* Magazin-Verlag, 1903.

Ellis, Havelock. *Sexual Inversion. Studies in the Psychology of Sex, Vol. 2.* 3rd ed. F.A. Davis, 1915.

Ellis, Havelock, and John Addington Symonds. *Sexual Inversion.* Wilson & MacMillan, 1897.

Freud, Sigmund. "The Sexual Aberrations." 1905. In *Three Essays on the Theory of Sexuality,* translated and edited by James Strachey, Basic Books, 2000.

Hammer, Wilhelm. *Die Tribadie Berlins.* Großstadt-Dokumente, vol. 20, H. Seemann, 1906.

Hirschfeld, Magnus. *Berlin's Third Sex.* 1904. Translated by James J. Conway, Rixdorf, 2017.

——, editor. *Jahrbuch für sexuelle Zwischenstufen.* Leipzig: Max Spohr Verlag, 1899–1903.

Hoffmann, Valeska. *Das vierte Geschlecht.* D.B. Wiemann, 1901.

Janitschek, Maria. *Die neue Eva.* Hermann Seemann Nachfolger, 1902.

Krafft-Ebing, Richard Freiherr von. *Psychopathia Sexualis.* Ferdinand Enke, 1886.

——. *Psychopathia Sexualis, 7th enlarged and revised edition.* Translated by Charles Gilbert Chaddock, The F.A. Davis Company, 1892.

——. *Psychopathia Sexualis, 12th edition.* Translated and edited by F.J. Rebman. Physicians and Surgeons Book Company, 1924.

——. *Über gesunde und kranke Nerven.* Verlag der H. Laupp'schen Buchhandlung, 1885.

Lange, Helene. "Grenzlinien zwischen Mann und Frau." 1897. In *Kampfzeiten: Aufsätze und Reden aus vier Jahrzehnten Vol. 2,* edited by Helene Lange, F.A. Herbig, 1928, pp. 197–216.

Lombroso, Cesare, and Guglielmo Ferrero. *Criminal Woman, the Prostitute, and the Normal Woman.* 1893. Translated by Nicole Hahn Rafter and Mary Gibson, Duke UP, 2004.

Marie-Madeleine [Baroness Gertrud von Puttkamer]. *Auf Kypros.* Vita, Deutsches Verlagshaus, 1900.

Mayne, Xavier [Edward Prime-Stevenson]. *The Intersexes: A History of Similisexualism as a Problem in Social Life.* Privately printed, 1908.

Meebold, Alfred. *Dr. Erna Redens Thorheit und Erkenntnis. Allerhand Volk,* edited by Alfred Meebold, Vita, 1900.

Mensch, Ella. *Auf Vorposten. Roman aus meiner Züricher Studienzeit.* Verlag der Frauen-Rundschau, 1903.

———. *Bilderstürmer in der Berliner Frauenbewegung.* Großstadt-Dokumente, vol. 26, H. Seemann, 1906.

Moll, Albert. *Die Conträre Sexualempfindung.* Fischers Medizinische Buchhandlung, 1891.

Niemann, August. *Zwei Frauen.* E. Piersons Verlag, 1901.

Nordau, Max. *Degeneration.* 1892. William Heinemann, 1898.

Roellig, Ruth. *Berlins lesbische Frauen.* Gebauer, 1928.

Rüling, Anna. "Welches Interesse hat die Frauenbewegung an der Lösung der homosexuellen Problems?" 1904. *Jahrbuch für sexuelle Zwischenstufen unter besonderer Berücksichtigung der Homosexualität,* vol. 7, 1905, pp. 130–51.

Schoenflies, Rosalie, editor. *Der Internationale Kongress fur Frauenwerke und Frauenbestrebungen in Berlin, 19. bis 26. September 1896: Eine Sammlung der auf dem Kongress gehaltenen Vortrage und Ansprachen.* H. Walther, 1897.

Symonds, John Addington. *A Problem in Greek Ethics, Being an Inquiry into the Phenomenon of Sexual Inversion.* Privately printed. 1883. Reprinted in Havelock Ellis and John Addington Symonds, *Sexual Inversion,* Wilson & MacMillan, 1897, pp. 163–251.

Trosse, Emma. *Der Konträrsexualismus inbezug auf Ehe und Frauenfrage.* Max Spohr Verlag, 1895.

———. *Ein Weib? Psychologisch-biographische Studie über eine Konträrsexuelle.* Max Spohr Verlag, 1897.

———. *Ist freie Liebe Sittenlosigkeit?* Max Spohr Verlag, 1897.

Ulrichs, Karl Heinrich. *Forschungen über das Räthsel der mannmännlichen Liebe. Erste Schrift "Vindex."* 1864. Max Spohr Verlag, 1898.

Wedekind, Frank. *Die Büchse der Pandora.* Die Insel, 1902.

———. *Erdgeist.* Langen, 1895.

Weininger, Otto. *Geschlecht und Charakter.* Wilhelm Braumüller, 1903.

Weirauch, Anna Elisabet. *Der Skorpion.* Askanischer Verlag, 1919, 1920, 1931.

Westermanns Illustrierte Deutsche Monatshefte, vol. 91, no. 2, November 1901, p. 303.

Westphal, Carl von. "Die konträre Sexualempfindung." *Archiv für Psychiatrie und Nervenkrankheiten, II.* August Hirschwald Verlag, 1869, pp. 73–108.

Winsloe, Christa. *Gestern und Heute [Ritter Nérestan].* Georg Marton, 1930.

———. *Das Mädchen Manuela. Der Roman von Mädchen in Uniform.* E.P. Tal & Co. Verlag, 1933.

Winsloe, Christa, and Friedrich Dammann. *Mädchen in Uniform.* Leontine Sagan, Reg. Deutsche Film-Gemeinschaft. 1931.
———. With Romy Schneider. *Mädchen in Uniform.* Géza Radványi, Reg. CCC/ Films Modernes. 1958.
Wolzogen, Ernst von. *Das dritte Geschlecht.* R. Eckstein, 1899.
———. *Im Frauenklub. Der Roman der Zwölf,* edited by Hermann Bahr, K.W. Mecklenburg, 1909.

Anthologies and Secondary Works on Mina Adelt-Duc, Lesbianism, Sexology, and the Women's Rights Movement in Turn-of-the-Century Germany; and Other Cited Works

Albisetti, James C. *Schooling German Girls and Women.* Princeton UP, 1989.
Allen, Ann Taylor. *Feminism and Motherhood in Germany, 1800–1914.* Rutgers UP, 1991.
Bauer, Heike. *English Literary Sexology: Translations of Inversion, 1860–1930.* Palgrave Macmillan, 2010.
———. *The Hirschfeld Archives: Violence, Death, and Modern Queer Culture.* Temple UP, 2017.
———, editor. *Sexology and Translation: Cultural and Scientific Encounters across the Modern World.* Temple UP, 2015.
———. "Theorizing Female Inversion: Sexology, Discipline, and Gender at the Fin de Siècle." *Journal of the History of Sexuality,* vol. 1, 2009, pp. 84–102.
Bauer, J. Edgar. "On the Nameless Love and Infinite Sexualities: John Henry Mackay, Magnus Hirschfeld and the Origins of the Sexual Emancipation Movement." *Journal of Homosexuality,* vol. 50, no. 1, 2005, pp. 1–26.
Beachy, Robert. *Gay Berlin: Birthplace of a Modern Identity.* Vintage, 2015.
Beccalosi, Chiara. *Female Sexual Inversion: Same-Sex Desires in Italian and British Sexology, 1870–1920.* Palgrave Macmillan, 2012.
Bei, Neda, et al., editors. *Das lila Wien um 1900: zur Ästhetik der Homosexualitäten.* Spuren, 1986.
Beutin, Heidi, Wolfgang Beutin, and Holger Malterer, editors. *Die Frau greift in die Politik: Schriftstellerinnen in Opposition, Revolution und Widerstand.* Peter Lang, 2010.
Bland, Caroline. "Through Science to Selfhood? The Early Generations of University Women in German Fiction." *Oxford German Studies,* vol. 45, no. 1, April 2016, pp. 45–61.
Breger, Claudia. "Feminine Masculinities: Scientific and Literary Representations of 'Female Inversion' at the Turn of the Twentieth

Century." *Journal of the History of Sexuality,* vol. 2, nos. 1–2, January/April 2005, pp. 76–106.

Claus, Doris. "Wenn die Freundin ihrer Freundin lila Veilchen schenkt: zum Selbstverständnis lesbischer Frauen am Anfang des 20. Jahrhunderts." In *Lulu, Lilith, Mona Lisa ... Frauenbilder der Jahrhundertwende,* edited by Irmgard Roebling, Centaurus, 1988, pp. 19–31.

Dobler, Jens. "*Der Liebe Lust und Leid der Frau zur Frau.* Ein wiederentdeckter Lesbenroman von 1895." *Forum Homosexualität und Literatur,* vol. 48, 2006, pp. 75–80.

Dünnebier, Anna, and Ursula Scheu. *Die Rebellion ist eine Frau: Anita Augspurg und Lida G. Heymann—Das schillerndste Paar der deutschen Frauenbewegung.* Hugendubel, 2002.

Eley, Geoff, Jennifer L. Jenkins, and Tracie Matysik, editors. *German Modernities from Wilhelm to Weimar: A Contest of Futures.* Bloomsbury, 2016.

Evans, Richard. *The Feminist Movement in Germany, 1894–1933.* London, 1976.

Faderman, Lillian. *Surpassing the Love of Men: Romantic Friendship and Love between Women from the Renaissance to the Present.* William Morrow & Co., 1981.

Faderman, Lillian, and Brigitte Eriksson, editors. *Lesbian-Feminism in Turn-of-the-Century-Germany.* Naiad, 1980.

Franzoi, Barbara. *At the Very Least She Pays the Rent: Women and German Industrialization, 1871–1914.* Greenwood P, 1985.

Fuechtner, Veronika, Douglas E. Haynes, and Ryan M. Jones, editors. *Global History of Sexual Science, 1880–1960.* U of California P, 2017.

Gluckman, Catherine Bailey. "Constructing Queer Female Identities in Late Realist German Fiction." *German Life and Letters,* vol. 65, no. 3, July 2012, pp. 318–32.

Göttert, Margit. *Macht und Eros. Frauenbeziehungen und weibliche Kultur um 1900—eine neue Perspektive auf Helen Lange und Gertrud Bäumer.* Ulrike Helmer Verlag, 2000.

Hacker, Hanna. *Frauen und Freundinnen. Studien zur "weiblichen Homosexualitat" am Beispiel Österreich 1870–1938.* Beltz, 1987.

——. "Tödlich, Humorvoll: Wien und die Wienerin in der lesbischen Literatur." *Das Lila Wien um 1900. Zur Ästhetik der Homosexualitäten,* edited by Neda Bei, Edition Spuren, 1986, pp. 21–35.

——. "Zonen des Verbotenen: Die lesbische Codierung von Kriminalität und Feminismus um 1900." *Que(e)r Denken: Weibliche /männliche Homosexualität und Wissenschaft,* edited by Barbara Hey, Ronald Pallier, and Roswith Roth, Studien Verlag, 1997, pp. 40–57.

Hacker, Hanna, and Manfred Lang. "Jenseits der Geschlechter, Zwischen Ihnen: Homosexualitäten im Wien der Jahrhundertwende." In *Das Lila Wien um 1900. Zur Ästhetik der Homosexualitäten*, edited by Neda Bei, Edition Spuren, 1986, pp. 8–20.

Hekma, Gert. "'A Female Soul in a Male Body': Sexual Inversion as Gender Inversion in Nineteenth-Century Sexology." *Third Sex, Third Gender: Beyond Sexual Dimorphism in Culture and History*, edited by Gilbert Herdt, Zone Books, 1994, pp. 213–40.

Henke, Christiane. *Anita Augspurg*. Rowohlt, 2000.

Herz, Rudolf, and Brigitte Bruns, editors. *Hof-Atelier Elvira 1887–1928. Ästheten, Emanzen, Aristokraten*. Fotomuseum im Münchner Stadtmuseum, 1985.

Jones, James W. *The Third Sex in German Literature from the Turn of the Century to 1933*. 1986. PhD dissertation, U of Wisconsin-Madison.

——. *"We of the Third Sex": Literary Representations of Homosexuality in Wilhelmine Germany*. Peter Lang, 1990.

Katz, Jonathan, editor. *Lesbianism and Feminism in Germany, 1895–1910*. Arno P, 1975.

Kokula, Ilse, editor. *Weibliche Homosexualität um 1900 in zeitgenössischen Dokumenten*. Frauenoffensive, 1981.

Leidinger, Christiane. "Anna Rüling: A Problemantic Foremother of Lesbian Herstory." *Journal of the History of Sexuality*, vol. 13, 2004, pp. 477–99.

——. *Keine Tochter aus gutem Hause—Johanna Elberskirchen (1864–1943)*. Universitätsverlag Konstanz, 2008.

Leng, Kirsten. "An 'Elusive' Phenomenon: Feminism, Sexology and the Female Sex Drive in Germany at the Turn of the 20th Century." *Centaurus: An International Journal of the History of Science and Its Cultural Aspects*, vol. 55, no. 2, May 2013, pp. 131–52.

——. "Permutations of the Third Sex: Sexology, Subjectivity, and Antimaternalist Feminism at the Turn of the Century." *Signs: Journal of Women in Culture and Society*, vol. 40, no. 1, 2014, pp. 227–54.

——. "Sex, Science, and Fin-de-Siècle Feminism: Johanna Elberskirchen Interprets *The Laws of Life*." *Journal of Women's History*, vol. 25, no. 3, 2013, pp. 38–61.

——. *Sexual Politics and Feminist Science: Women Sexologists in Germany, 1900–1933*. Cornell UP, 2018.

Livy. *History of Rome. Volume IX: Books 31–34*. Translated by Evan T. Sage, Loeb Classic Library, Harvard UP, 1935.

Lorey, Christoph. "Frauen-Zimmerwelten: Die räumliche Einbindung weiblicher Sexualität in den Romanen *Sind es Frauen* von

Aimée Duc und *Das Mädchen Manuela* von Christa Winsloe."
Forum Homosexualität und Literatur, vol. 39, 2001, pp. 27–44.

Lybeck, Marti M. *Desiring Emancipation: New Women and Homosexuality in Germany, 1890–1933*. SUNY P, 2014.

Mancini, Elena. *Magnus Hirschfeld and the Quest for Sexual Freedom: A History of the First International Sexual Freedom Movement*. Palgrave Macmillan, 2010.

Martin, Biddy. "Extraordinary Homosexuals and the Fear of Being Ordinary." *differences*, vol. 6, nos. 2–3, 1994, pp. 100–25.

Matysik, Tracie. "In the Name of the Law: The 'Female Homosexual' and the Criminal Code in Fin de Siècle Germany." *Journal of the History of Sexuality*, vol. 13, no. 1, January 2004, pp. 26–48.

Mazón, Patricia M. "'Fräulein Doktor': Literary Images of the First Female University Students in Fin-de-Siècle Germany." *Women in German Yearbook*, vol. 16, 2001, pp. 129–50.

——. *Gender and the Modern Research University: The Admission of Women to German Higher Education, 1865–1914*. Stanford UP, 2003.

Meder, Stephan, Andrea Czelk, and Arne Duncker, editors. *Die Rechtsstellung der Frau um 1900: Eine kommentierte Quellensammlung*. Böhlau, 2010.

Muellner, Beth. "The Photographic Enactment of the Early New Woman in 1890s German Women's Bicycling Magazines." *Women in German Yearbook*, vol. 22, 2006, pp. 167–88.

Oosterhuis, Harry. *Stepchildren of Nature: Krafft-Ebing, Psychiatry, and the Making of Sexual Identity*. U of Chicago P, 2000.

Rich, Adrienne. "Compulsory Heterosexuality and Lesbian Existence." *Signs*, vol. 5, no. 4, Summer 1980, pp. 631–60.

Richardsen, Ingvild. *Evas Töchter: Münchner Schriftstellerinnen und die moderne Frauenbewegung 1894–1933*. Volk Verlag, 2018.

Roebling, Irmgard, editor. *Lulu, Lilith, Mona Lisa—: Frauenbilder der Jahrhundertwende*. Frauen in Geschichte und Gesellschaft. Centaurus-Verlagsgesellschaft, 1989.

Rowold, Katharina. *The Educated Woman: Minds, Bodies, and Women's Higher Education in Britain, Germany, and Spain, 1865–1914*. Routledge Research in Gender and History. Routledge, 2009.

Schmersahl, Katrin. "'Sind es Frauen?' Zur Reaktion von Frauen auf antifeministische Topoi." *Denken heisst Grenzen überschreiten. Beiträge aus der sozialhistorischen Frauen- und Geschlechterforschung*, edited by Elke Kleinau et al., von Bockel Verlag, 1995, pp. 181–91.

Schoppmann, Claudia. *Der Skorpion. Frauenliebe in der Weimarer Republik*. FrühlingsErwachen, 1985.

——. "Vom Kaiserreich bis zum Ende des Zweiten Weltkriegs—Eine

Einführung." *In Bewegung bleiben. 100 Jahre Politik, Kultur und Geschichte von Lesben,* edited by Gabriele Dennert, Christiane Leidinger, and Franziska Rauchut, collaborator Stefanie Soine, Querverlag, 2007, pp. 12–16.

Sigusch, Volkmar. "The Sexologist Albert Moll—between Sigmund Freud and Magnus Hirschfeld." *The International Journal for the History of Medicine and Related Sciences,* vol. 56, no. 2, April 2012, pp. 184–200.

Taylor, Mara. *Diagnosing Deviants: The Figure of the Lesbian in Sexological and Literary Discourses, 1860–1931.* 2010. PhD dissertation, U of Pennsylvania.

Taylor, Michael Thomas, Annette F. Timm, and Rainer Herrn, editors. *Not Straight from Germany: Sexual Publics and Sexual Politics since Magnus Hirschfeld.* U of Michigan P, 2017.

Tobin, Robert Deam. *Peripheral Desires: The German Discovery of Sex.* U of Pennsylvania P, 2015.

Weeks, Jeffrey. *Against Nature: Essay on History, Sexuality and Identity.* Rivers Oram P, 1991.

Whisnant, Clayton John. *Queer Identities and Politics in Germany: A History, 1880–1945.* Harrington Park P, 2016.

From the Publisher

A name never says it all, but the word "Broadview" expresses a good deal of the philosophy behind our company. We are open to a broad range of academic approaches and political viewpoints. We pay attention to the broad impact book publishing and book printing has in the wider world; for some years now we have used 100% recycled paper for most titles. Our publishing program is internationally oriented and broad-ranging. Our individual titles often appeal to a broad readership too; many are of interest as much to general readers as to academics and students.

Founded in 1985, Broadview remains a fully independent company owned by its shareholders—not an imprint or subsidiary of a larger multinational.

For the most accurate information on our books (including information on pricing, editions, and formats) please visit our website at www.broadviewpress.com. Our print books and ebooks are also available for sale on our site.

broadview press
www.broadviewpress.com

This book is made of paper from well-managed FSC® - certified forests, recycled materials, and other controlled sources.